MW01173991

Strong ...
worry," Logan said. "I've got you."

She clung to his neck as he gathered her closer. She could feel his heart beat against her chest, or was that hers? Random thoughts popped in and out. How had he reached her so fast? Did he think she was clumsy? Too heavy?

Pathetic. He'd saved her, and all she could think about was her weight. Still...

She squirmed in his arms. "Thank you, but you can put me down."

"And blow my one chance to rescue a beautiful damsel in distress? Not a chance. Besides, we're almost there."

Although the bagpipes were louder and she could hear the haunting notes of a flute, the mist was as dense as ever. "How can you tell?" she said.

She felt a rumble of laughter rise in his chest. "It's a guess. I haven't a clue."

Praise for Pam Binder

"Readers will be drawn in by Pam Binder's magic touch."

~Romantic Times

~*~

"Light hearted, yet engaging."

~Publishers Weekly

~*~

"Delightful twists and turns."

~Reader to Reader Reviews

~*~

"...a truly delightful and heartwarming romance."

~American Online Romance Fiction Forum

~*~

"This was my first, but definitely not my last, Pam Binder book."

~The Romance Reader's Connection

~*~

"Magical. A timeless love story."

~Stella Cameron

~*~

**Other Books in the Matchmaker Café Series
by Pam Binder
available soon from The Wild Rose Press, Inc.**
A BRIDE FOR A DAY
A VALENTINE FOR EMMA
LOVE POEM
CHRISTMAS KNIGHT
IRISH LOVE SONG

Match Made in the Highlands

by

Pam Binder

Matchmaker Café Series, Book 1

Match Made in the Highlands

Cover Art by *Debbie Taylor*

The Wild Rose Press, Inc.
PO Box 708
Adams Basin, NY 14410-0708
Visit us at www.thewildrosepress.com

Publishing History
First Fantasy Rose Edition, 2016
Print ISBN 978-1-5092-0880-7
Digital ISBN 978-1-5092-0881-4

Matchmaker Café Series, Book 1
Published in the United States of America

Dedication

To my beautiful sister: Marilyn Louise Todd.
Together we keep the memory of
our mother's love and generous spirit alive.

Acknowledgments

Thank you to everyone who helped make
the Matchmaker Café Series a reality.
First to my wonderful author friends,
the talented Gerri Russell and Sabrina York,
who encouraged me to keep writing;
to Mimi Munk, whose insights and feedback I trust;
to my agent, Michelle Grajkowksi,
for her continued support;
to my fantastic new editor at The Wild Rose Press,
Nan Swanson;
and of course to the amazing Rhonda Penders,
who made this dream come true.
Thank you all.

Chapter One

Snow danced around the black taxicab like secrets begging to be told as Irene Redmond re-read the last entry in her mother's diary. The handwriting was crisp and orderly, so like her mother, but the words made no sense. Why was this place so important, and who was Connor?

"We're here, lass," the driver said. "Stirling Castle."

The castle looked dark and foreboding. It was a fortress built on a volcanic outcrop, meant to keep people out, not welcome the curious. Irene smoothed the pages of her mother's diary as though touching the love-worn paper could unlock her mother's secrets. Stalling for time, Irene remained in the cab and slipped the diary into her tote bag. She glanced through the window at the swirling snowflakes that turned the grey morning into shades of white. Their confusion mirrored her emotions, or maybe she was jetlagged, or both.

Her mother's diary, addressed to her two daughters, had arrived after her death. It had hinted at a secret past, a secret love, with the declaration that a Scottish castle, this one outside in the snowstorm, to be exact, held the answers. Her mother would have known that Irene would never be able to leave a puzzle unsolved.

The ten-hour plane trip from Seattle to London

hadn't been so bad. It was navigating through the Christmas holiday rush at the train station when she was sleep-deprived that had proven the biggest challenge. If she'd been smart, she'd have taken a week off instead of trying to do this all in four days, but one of her clients had a court date scheduled.

"Lass?"

Irene blinked and refocused on handing the taxi driver his fee. "Are you sure Stirling Castle is open today?"

He smoothed down a salt-and-pepper beard and smiled so widely his eyes twinkled, reminding Irene of jolly old St. Nick. "Like heather in the Highlands," he said, "and mist over the moors, Stirling Castle is always open on Christmas Eve. But if you have second thoughts…"

His question hung in the air as her heart pounded against her chest. She'd changed her mind about this trip at least a hundred times. Her partners at the law firm had told her she shouldn't be away from her clients over the holidays and had even brought in her cheating ex-fiancé to help make their case. Their strategy had backfired. It was time she unraveled her mother's secrets.

"Now or never," she said under her breath.

Irene gathered her belongings and opened the car door. The faint sound of church bells drifted toward her from the town below and swirled together with icy snowflakes. Perhaps this wouldn't be so bad. A blast of winter air pushed against her as she stepped outside, spoiling the moment. She shivered and pulled the hood of her coat over her head. "It's freezing."

The taxicab driver's laughter shook his whole

body. "When you're with the right person, you won't notice the cold. I'll be here to pick you up after the matchmaker tour."

She shut the door before what he'd said registered. "Wait," she called out. "You must be mistaken. I'm here for the history tour. Is that the same thing?"

Laughter clung to the air as he pulled away from the curb and disappeared down the winding road.

Chapter Two

Stirling Castle in Scotland was a blend of the ancient world and the new. White lights outlined the windows and castle entrance, while snow only partially covered the war-pocked grey walls. It was the perfect backdrop for a Christmas card.

The snow picked up speed.

It swirled around Irene as though the storm had singled her out for personal torment as she waited in line to buy her ticket for the noon tour. She hated waiting in line. Her partners were right. This was a dumb idea, but if she left, her sister would never let her hear the end of it.

Resigned, she glanced toward the front of the line to see what was taking so long. Three men who looked to be in their mid-thirties were ahead of her. They wore ill-fitting brown tunics belted over leggings, as though they'd planned to attend a medieval or Renaissance faire. Their costumes were made from synthetic cloth and their belts were black plastic. Their spiky hair, agitated gestures, and closely spaced eyes reminded Irene of mice who'd escaped their cage. It was obvious by their weaving and slurred speech that they'd started celebrating the holiday season a little early.

Two of the men flirted with the young woman inside the ticket booth, while the shortest of the trio chose to include Irene, pairing a wink and a leer together with comical results. When his advances were ignored, he turned back to the booth. He addressed the young woman as Fiona and tried to convince her to sell them tickets.

Even from a short distance away, Irene could tell they were losing their argument. Fiona's hair was pulled back into a ponytail, and she wore white fake bunny fur earmuffs and black-framed glasses. But despite her sweet appearance, she looked like she had a spine made of steel.

"You were told never to return," Fiona said. All three of the men talked at the same time, each in turn offering her triple the price of the tickets. Fiona peered over the rims of her glasses at the three men and said slowly, "Go. Away."

They seemed startled but didn't argue as they turned and headed toward the castle.

When Irene reached the ticket counter, she rolled her eyes toward the men and received a mirrored response and a nod from Fiona. "They're idiots," Irene said.

"Aye, and soon to get what they deserve, if I was to put a wager on it." She paused. "If you don't mind me saying, you have the look of Ireland about you, all dark hair and green eyes."

Irene accepted the familiar compliment. It felt good to remember happier times. "I was born on St. Patrick's Day, and until first grade, I thought my name was Shamrock."

Fiona's laugh was as warm as her expression. "Ah, a family with a sense of humor. That's a blessing." There was a slight hesitation. "Will that be one ticket?"

The question bothered Irene less and less these

days. Perhaps it was because she was taking seriously her mother's advice. She had said you had to be happy being alone before you could be happy in the company of another person.

Irene nodded and pushed the exact amount of money through the window slit.

"Our tours are running a little late," Fiona said as she handed Irene a ticket. "If you're cold, you can wait inside the castle. The Matchmaker Café serves yummy hot cocoa."

The word "matchmaker" hung in the air. Irene had had her fill of friends offering to set her up on coffee dates or blindsiding her with their friends or relatives showing up unannounced at a dinner party. She'd even experimented with online dating services. The sites suggested that a new relationship would heal a failed one. It had made her feel only lonelier.

Irene shook her head slowly. "They won't try to do any...you know..." She cleared her throat. "I'm only in Scotland until tomorrow evening. Besides, I don't have time for a relationship." She clamped her mouth shut and folded the ticket, trying to figure out why she was sharing so much with a perfect stranger. That was not like her.

Fiona's laughter drifted out from the booth. "It's good you're in Scotland, then. Time is a curious thing here. But be off before you catch a cold. I wouldn't want you missing our tour." She leaned forward, and her features warmed as though she were sitting close to a cheery fire. "And remember, it's just hot cocoa. What could possibly happen?"

A gust of wind shoved Irene's hood off her head. She pulled it back into place. "I didn't see the café when I arrived. Where did you say it's located?"

Fiona opened her window a little wider and a warm breath of air weaved toward Irene as Fiona pointed toward the three-story-high doors to Stirling Castle. On the wall a short distance away was an arched entrance with the words Matchmaker Café spelled out in white blinking lights.

"It looks innocent enough," Irene said, shoving her gloves back onto her cold fingers.

Fiona drew back into her snug booth. "Be sure to ask for sprinkles." With that, she closed the shutters over the ticket window and the booth went dark.

Chapter Three

A Christmas wreath made of white lavender and sprigs of pine and fir hung over the entrance to the Matchmaker Café. Irene opened the door with only a slight turn of the handle. Celtic music played in the background. The notes of the flute echoed as though played in a vast cavern and tugged at her memories.

She hovered on the threshold, feeling like an outsider observing a play. Well-loved leather chairs were pulled close to a roaring fire, and lampshades were fringed with crystal beads. Plush velvet-draped wooden chairs hugged tables that were topped with red and green votive candles. Despite the cold outside, the mood in the café was warm and inviting.

The café was crowded with those waiting for the tours to begin. Couples snuggled in various corners drinking hot spiced cider, a group of women Irene guessed might be writers discussed plotlines for their novels, while at another table a family—mother, father, and young son—sat bent over their cell phones and tablets. Two men and a woman about Irene's age were grouped in one corner, laughing over a shared joke. Someone who had the look of a tour guide instructed families on the history of the castle and its connection to William Wallace and the movie *Braveheart*.

The same trio of men Irene had seen earlier at the ticket booth argued with their waitress in the same manner they had with Fiona. They looked even more alike in the café than they had outside in the storm, with their moon-shaped faces, narrow eyes, and red-splotched cheeks.

The woman they were harassing looked even less impressed than Fiona had. Her straight blond hair was piled on top of her head in a loose knot and threatened to escape every time she shook her head. She wore a white sweater and wool slacks that reminded Irene of the shade of fresh snow, as well as charm-like earrings so long they skimmed her shoulders.

"We don't serve alcohol at the Matchmaker Café," the woman said as she folded her arms. "But you could check if the castle's restaurant is still open. If my sister wouldn't sell you tickets, she had her reasons. You need to leave."

The tallest of the three shoved past his comrades to hover over her. Irene couldn't hear what he said, but the woman first cringed, then pressed her lips together and turned to leave. Before she had a chance to get away, he grabbed her arm.

Irene ground her teeth. How dare they bully her? She moved toward them, but before she had the chance to intervene, a man appeared out of nowhere and stepped between the waitress and the bullies.

He towered over the trio as he clamped his hand on the shoulder of the one who'd threatened the woman. His knuckles whitened as he leveled his gaze on all three. He seemed unconcerned that he was outnumbered. She didn't doubt he could defend himself, but he was not the only one in the café.

She appreciated his intervention, but she'd seen firsthand in her court cases what happened when fights spiraled out of control. The innocent sometimes got injured. Irene moved closer until she was a few feet away, keeping her voice calm and under control. "There are children in the café. Do you really want them to witness a fight, or worse, accidentally get hurt?"

He turned toward her in slow motion. His jawline was as rigid as stone and his eyes the shade of blue ice. Time held its breath. He pulled his gaze away as he scanned the room, focusing on the families. He paused on an elderly, distinguished couple sitting in a far corner.

When his gaze returned to hers, there was a slight nod and an upward turn on the corner of his mouth. Was he smiling? "You're a brave one," he said with a faint Scottish brogue. "But I've got this." He refocused on the man he still held by the shoulder and his comrades, then said something under his breath. They snapped to attention, tripping over each other as they raced outside.

The man glanced once more in her direction and gave a nod before joining the elderly couple.

It looked like few if any had witnessed the exchange, or else they'd chosen not to get involved. In either case, everything went on as though nothing had happened.

The waitress who'd been harassed by the trio let out a long breath and approached Irene. "Whew, well, that sure got the heart pumping. Normally the guests who come here are well behaved. Would you like a table," she said with a grin, "or would you like me to call you a taxi so you can make a hasty exit?"

Irene returned the smile. "I'm fine. I don't give up that easily." She cast a glance toward the rescuer. "Do you know what he said?"

The waitress bit back a smile. "He gave them a choice. Stay in the café and he'd use them as practice dummies, or leave. I overheard one of the men say he recognized the guy as a rugby player, which, given his appearance, is not surprising. Not everyone would have stepped in to help these days."

Irene couldn't help but smile as she followed the waitress to a table not far from the rugby player. "Good for him."

"I couldn't agree more. My name's Bridget, by the way."

"I'm Irene," she said, holding out her hand. She was starting to feel more relaxed.

"Very pleased to meet you. Hot cocoa, then? You look chilled to the bone."

Irene nodded as she settled on the bench seat and began to unwrap her scarf. She paused. "Oh, could you add sprinkles?"

Bridget turned around so suddenly her earrings sang like wind chimes.

Irene pulled the scarf slowly from her neck. "Sorry. That sounded silly. Never mind. Sprinkles are for children. I'm not sure why I asked," Irene said in a rush, fingering the snowflake charm on her necklace. "The young woman at the ticket booth suggested it, and for some reason it sounded fun. No worries if you don't have any. Plus, sprinkles are for children."

Bridget's smile broadened. "Ah, now, that would be my sister Fiona who suggested the sprinkles. We have a saying in our family: never lose the child within. I'll be sure to add a generous dash on your whipped cream. I love your locket, by the way. Did you purchase it in Scotland?"

Irene felt her voice catch. "It's not a locket. It was actually a set of earrings our mother converted into pendants for my sister and me a long time ago." Irene held it toward Bridget. "See, the snowflake is soldered to a silver disk."

Bridget raised an eyebrow. "Of course. My mistake. I'll bring your hot cocoa straight away."

Chapter Four

The atmosphere in the café held a note of quiet expectation as Irene cupped the warm mug of cocoa. The whipped cream was so thick it looked like a swirl of ice cream. As promised, there was a generous topping of chocolate and sugar sprinkles. The room was so hushed, she imagined she could hear snowflakes drift over the windowpanes. More people had entered the café, but there was a subdued quality about them, as though they were in church.

The rugby player had joined the elderly couple at a table not far away from hers. The older gentleman fed soup to his wife, even though his hand was so large he had a difficult time holding the small spoon. Although his wife opened her mouth to accept the broth, her eyes were vacant, and her skin was the color of parchment. But the tender, loving expression the man gifted his wife took Irene's breath away.

She sighed as she drew the mug of cocoa to her lips, savoring the taste of the rich whipped cream and sprinkles. A low chuckle drew her attention back to the rugby player and his parents. He caught her gaze and smiled at her. As his smile broadened, he touched his fingers to his nose and then his mouth.

She felt the instant warmth of a blush spread from her neck to her face. Was he flirting with her? She cast a furtive glace over her shoulder to make sure he was looking at her and then it registered.

Irene tested her tongue on her upper lip. It was covered in cream. She snatched up a napkin, feeling the heat of the blush deepen. She ducked her head to the side and wiped the cream off her face. He'd been staring at her. She sat up a little straighter. When she turned back, his attention had been drawn to his parents. The moment was lost.

What are you doing? Irene took another sip of cocoa, careful to avoid wearing the whipped cream this time. *You vowed to give up on relationships. Remember? Besides, knights in shining armor who are also devoted to their parents are either married or engaged. You are here to unlock your mother's secrets. You are not here for romance.*

With that thought in mind, she reached for the diary in her tote bag. The cloth cover was the shade of meadow grass and so worn it was held together by rubber bands and oversized binder clips. Newspaper and travel magazine clippings were pasted on many of the pages, and a few had drawings or quotes. There were even recipes and photographs.

Her mother had touched these pages. Holding the diary and re-reading her words made Irene feel closer to the memories. The three of them, she, her twin sister Louise, and their mother, used to say that anything was possible as long as they stuck together. Even after their mother had married, fifteen years ago, the bond between them hadn't wavered.

Louise was the artist in the family. She'd leave slips of paper around the house with lines of poetry beneath her sketches. When Irene announced she was going to law school, Louse had said she was going to be a *New York Times* bestselling children's book author. They'd both accomplished their goals.

Her sister had wanted to come along on this trip but had just found out she was pregnant. Irene was doing this for both of them.

Irene felt her breath catch in her throat as she opened the diary and turned to the entry she'd read in the taxicab.

Dear Diary,

One of my favorite movies as a child was Brigadoon *with Gene Kelly and Cyd Charisse. I always wondered what it would be like to discover a love as strong as theirs. And then I visited Scotland, the place where this wonderful legend took place, and met Connor. The last lines in the movie seem to have been written with us in mind: "…when you love someone deeply enough anything is possible. Even miracles."*

"That's beautiful."

Startled, Irene lifted her gaze toward Bridget, then quickly swiped at her wet cheeks and tucked the diary back into her tote bag. "It belonged to my mother. She passed away." Irene pulled the tote bag closer to her on the bench. Now why'd she say that? It was unlike her to share so much with strangers. She sat up straighter. "The hot cocoa is wonderful. Thank you."

Bridget's smile broadened. "It's a family secret. Our mother used to say she added a dash of magic before it was served."

"My mother said things like that too, when she baked." Irene tightened her hold on her bag. "Whoa, not sure why I'm sharing. I blame the jet lag. I'm usually not this talkative."

Bridget's laughter was as soft as a whisper. "It is

15

understandable. The memories of those we've loved are always closest to us this time of year. When you've finished your cocoa, you can proceed to the line. Our sister, Lady Roselyn, will explain everything you'll need to know about the tour once you're inside." She handed Irene an antique-looking key with a red velvet ribbon attached. "This is for the locker where you can store your clothes after you've changed into a costume appropriate for thirteenth-century Scotland."

"Costume?"

Bridget pushed the key closer to Irene. "Fiona must have forgotten to tell you. She's been a little distracted of late. She was recently betrothed. She…" Bridget waved aside whatever else she had intended to say. "Anyway, dressing in the clothes of the period enhances the adventure. It's actually my favorite part. The tour becomes more than a museum-like experience." Bridget hesitated. "But if you'd rather not, you'll still enjoy our more traditional tour. However, you should make your decision soon. Those with the keys are lining up on the far right."

The café had indeed come to life. The families, along with about a dozen others, had decided against the costume option and were headed to an entrance on the opposite side of the room. Everyone else was navigating to the men's and women's changing rooms Bridget had indicated.

Irene had traveled to Scotland to get away from everything and everybody, in order to find answers. That was what this Christmas pilgrimage was all about. Shedding her modern clothes seemed like a great idea, if only for a few hours. She gulped down her cocoa and grabbed the key before she changed her mind.

Chapter Five

The changing room was a stark contrast to the café, evoking the rich textures and colors of a forest at dusk. Candles and an amber fire cast their glow over gowns and headpieces. Irene guessed they were replicas of thirteenth-century costumes. Clothes in shades of berry red, pine needle green, and starlight silver were draped over chairs, a sofa, and hung from gilded dividers.

A young woman about Irene's age, with short clipped dark hair and a face that reminded Irene of a cute pixie elf, snatched a bundle of gowns and disappeared behind one of the partitions. The rugby player's mother was the only other person in the room, and she seemed as confused as Irene felt.

"I think they want us to choose a costume," Irene said as she moved toward the older woman.

The woman's brow furrowed. Irene fought the impulse to reach out and guide her toward a chair. Irene didn't know how the woman would react to a stranger. She looked lost.

"Hello, I don't believe we've met. My name is Irene."

The woman turned toward her slowly and focused on Irene's outstretched hand, but there was little or no understanding behind her eyes. Irene wondered if she even knew that she was in a castle, let alone on a tour that required costumes.

17

Candle flames rippled as a woman entered and stepped between Irene and the older woman. The only splash of color on the newcomer's midnight-blue gown was a red plaid sash draped over one shoulder. Her hair was pulled back in a severe bun covered with a starched veil, but rebel strands of hair had escaped to frame her face, hinting at a thick mane of curls. She reminded Irene of her firm's principal stockholder, who wore only blacks and charcoal grey and after a lifetime of making difficult decisions considered smiling a foreign concept.

The woman who'd entered folded her hands in a tight grip at her waist. "Good. You are all here. I apologize for being late. Business concerns. You may address me as Lady Roselyn. I believe you all have met my sisters, Fiona and Bridget. And as you can see, we have provided costumes in a variety of sizes and shades. Most of our guests begin with a conservative choice and then change later into formal attire for our Christmas Eve ball at midnight. There is no sense starting out like peacocks. What would come after? A gown fit only for a Mardi Gras float?"

"I happen to adore Mardi Gras," said the pixie-faced young woman as she emerged from behind the divider. She wore a form-fitting red silk gown that complimented her complexion to perfection as she twirled around in a circle to show it off. "In New Orleans they know how to make a good first impression."

"As do you, Julia," Lady Roselyn said with the hint of a smile. "I stand corrected. You have made an exceptional choice. Now for introductions." She turned first toward the rugby player's mother. "Ann," Lady

Roselyn said softly, "we are honored you've joined us, and we have your selections set aside." Lady Roselyn hesitated for a moment as though waiting for a response. When there was none, she continued, "Julia is the lovely woman in the red dress, and Irene is to my right. Remember that in the thirteenth century it was the fashion for a lady to wear a head covering. We have a selection of simple veils, such as the one I'm wearing, or the more elaborate, conical-style hats. Oh, and two of our rules is that we address each other on a first name basis only, and that we never, ever, ask guests their occupations."

"Rules," Julia said, with an exaggerated sigh. "Don't you and your sisters ever get tired of them?"

Lady Roselyn ignored Julia as she guided Ann over to a selection of gowns with matching hats and veils. "Rules are what make the tour experience operate smoothly. You should be pleased there is not a rule against our guests returning time and time again."

The tension between them mounted into a good old-fashioned stare-down contest.

Ann broke the silence as she flung one of the head coverings to the ground. "I hate hats."

Everyone in the room was too stunned to react. Ann hadn't said one word to anyone since she'd arrived. Irene had never thought it was because Ann couldn't talk. The more likely reason was that she hadn't had the desire. Her mother had also behaved that way toward the end.

Lady Roselyn regained her composure first and reached up to unpin her veil. She then tossed it aside. "I loathe them as well. I never understood the appeal. Very confining. I proclaim that, from this moment on, hats and veils are optional."

Lady Roselyn's dramatics seemed to calm Ann. She sat back down and folded her hands in her lap, resuming her distant gaze. Lady Roselyn kept her attention on Ann for a few more moments before turning back to Irene and Julia. "Now, if there aren't any more questions, you are free to make your selections."

Chapter Six

In the end, Irene chose a pale grey gown with a matching pointed hat and starched veil. She'd debated about wearing a head covering, partially since it appeared she would be the only one. But when she tried it on as an experiment, she knew it was perfect for her. A hat and veil served a dual purpose, as far as she was concerned. They contained her unruly long curls and helped make her feel invisible. The downside was that the costume made it hard for her to turn her head. Evidently that was the price of being in fashion, for a woman in the thirteenth century.

Lady Roselyn had brought out many gowns for Ann, but the only color she would agree to wear was black. She settled on one with long fitted sleeves. Despite the severity, it brought out Ann's sky-blue eyes and highlighted the beauty of her snow-white hair.

"You look lovely," Irene whispered to Ann.

For a moment Irene thought she noticed a flicker of life behind Ann's eyes, but as quickly as it had appeared, it vanished.

"Are we ready, ladies?" Lady Roselyn announced. When everyone nodded, she continued, "As Bridget may have told some of you, when you pass through these doors, you will enter Stirling Castle as it was in 1297. To assist you in having the best possible experience, we have devised a few rules."

Julia groaned, and Irene pinched her lips together to keep from smiling. Lady Roselyn didn't miss a step. She gave both Julia and Irene a glance that would have melted a glacier.

"As I was saying. Rules. One, no cell phones or modern electronic devices of any kind. You can leave your belongings in the lockers located near the double doors. Two, stay in character at all times. You are guests for the laird's daughter's wedding. The bride's name is Caitlin. Three, do not mention that you are visiting from the twenty-first century. If asked, you are allowed to say Italy or France or even Britain. The Americas haven't been colonized yet. Last, and the most important, you must not try to leave until the tour has ended and my sisters and I have escorted you back to these rooms. My counterpart, Liam MacDonald, has already counseled the men on these rules. One more thing before we leave," she said as she moved toward the double doors. "We will be traveling down a steep flight of stairs, so please be very careful."

As Irene gathered her clothes and tote bag and started putting them away, Julia slipped in next to her.

"I thought I wouldn't be nervous," Julia said, "but I'm shaking like a leaf. Are you nervous?"

The comment caught Irene off guard. Of course she was nervous. She might discover a secret about her mother she didn't like. But this was just a tour. Why was Julia nervous?

She started to ask, but Lady Roselyn clapped her hands for their attention.

"Come, ladies," Lady Roselyn said. "Our tour is about to begin." She flung opened the thick oak double doors that were each covered with images of Scottish thistles. Mist and the far-off sound of bagpipes filled the entrance.

Irene stepped up to the threshold and hesitated. Did she really want to do this? Maybe her ex was right and she was just chasing dreams. Her mother didn't have secrets, just a vivid imagination.

Julia threaded her arm through Irene's. "We shouldn't keep Lady Roselyn waiting."

"I thought you were nervous," Irene said.

Julia smiled. "I am, but sometimes you have to take a leap."

****

On the threshold, mist swirled around Irene's feet as thick and clingy as white cotton candy. The distant bagpipes vibrated through her and conjured images of another time and place. Momentarily drawn into the fantasy and excitement of pretending to visit another century, she hesitated and stifled a laugh. Whoever was responsible for arranging this tour had a real skill for the dramatic.

"What are we waiting for," she whispered to Julia.

Julia shook her head slowly. Her eyes were focused straight ahead, and Irene had the impression the woman hadn't heard a word she'd said.

Out of the corner of her eye, Irene saw men emerge from a room next to hers. One was Ann's son, another Ann's husband, plus two more men Irene didn't recognize. Ann's husband and son were engaged in a heated debate. Irene caught bits and pieces. Ann was missing. The son put his hand on his father's arm as though to restrain him, and then gazed toward Irene.

"We didn't see my mother leave," he shouted over to her. "Would you mind checking on her?"

"Not at all," Irene said and retraced her steps.

When she stepped back over the threshold, the changing area looked different. Instead of a large room, draped with gowns, ribbons and hats, it resembled a maze. Of course, everything had happened in such a blur, maybe she'd not paid close attention.

Irene called out Ann's name. When there wasn't a response, she moved in farther and raised her voice. "Ann? Are you in here?"

There was always the chance Ann had changed her mind and returned to the café. Then Irene remembered Ann's vacant expression. She'd recognized the worry in the father's and son's eyes. She'd seen that same look in the expression of one of her clients when he'd talked about his mother's failing memory and the doctor's diagnosis. The more troubling possibility was that Ann had left the café and was now wandering out in the freezing cold.

Irene plunged into the center corridor of the maze-like room with its bank of lockers. "Ann? Please answer me. Your son's worried. He asked me to find you."

From a short distance away, Irene heard a locker shut, then a few mumbled words. Irene rushed toward the sound. Ann was sitting on the bench as though she were waiting for someone to fetch her. Beside her was Irene's diary.

"How did you…" Irene began.

Ann stood and handed Irene her diary. "You'll need this." She then walked past Irene.

"Okay, that was strange," Irene said. She clutched the diary and scrambled after the woman. For some reason, Ann seemed to know exactly where she was going.

At the threshold, Ann's son was waiting for them. He scooped his mother into an embrace and gave her a gentle hug before releasing her. "Mother, are you sure you want to do the tour? I know it was your idea, but we can always do it another time."

She lifted her head toward him. Her eyes focused for a brief moment, then clouded over as she turned and walked toward her husband's waiting arms.

"I guess that was a yes," he said under his breath.

Lady Roselyn appeared out of the mist. "There you all are. We must hurry," she said in a frantic voice. "We are late."

Ann's son held back and extended his hand to Irene. "I'm Logan, by the way. Thank you for helping my mother. Where did you find her?"

"She was sitting in the locker area. It was odd. It was almost as though she was waiting for me."

He lifted an eyebrow, adjusting the leather belt and sword that hung at an angle at his hips. "This tour has been odd from the beginning. It's not at all what I expected, and I'm starting to think this is only the beginning. You're dressed as a high-born lady from the thirteenth century, and I look like King Arthur." There was laughter and then another smile. "I'm loving it."

She grinned, drawn to the smile that lit up his face. All the men she'd dated treated laughter as a sign of weakness. He wore it as naturally as others would wear a pair of socks. "I think you mean you're dressed like Scotland's leader William Wallace."

"You're a history geek."

"Guilty."

"People," Lady Roselyn shouted, clapping her hands. "Hurry, or we'll leave you behind."

Chapter Seven

Irene held back as Logan disappeared into a mist filled with twinkling lights that danced like thousands of fireflies in time with the haunting notes of bagpipes. Logan had suggested that he'd thought the tour odd. She knew why he'd said that. How many tour directors asked people to dress in costume? Not many, was her guess, as they'd fear open rebellion. Most adults thought they were too grown up. The last one she'd worn was when she was a child in grammar school. Her mother had loved making costumes.

The gowns Lady Roselyn provided reminded her of the style and colors of dresses her mother had spent months sewing for the three of them. While most children dressed as ghosts or action heroes or heroines for Halloween, she and her sister had looked like they'd fit into the court of a medieval king or queen. Those were happy memories. Irene smoothed her hand over her sleeve. She loved the feel of the silk, but the dull color didn't seem right. The dresses her mother had made were more vibrant, more alive.

The bagpipes grew louder, as though beckoning her to hurry. She picked up her skirts. She changed her mind. She didn't think anything was odd. Quite to the contrary.

Irene quickened her steps as she plunged into the mist. She heard voices over the music, so at least the tour group hadn't gone very far, but the mist was so thick it was like being caught in a blinding snowstorm. Visibility was near zero.

"Concentrate," she said aloud. Her headdress prevented her from turning easily, and her gown was too long—or she was too short, which at five foot ten seemed unlikely. Yet another indication that she'd chosen incorrectly.

The first step caught her off guard. Irene wobbled back and forth, feeling disoriented. She thrust her arms out like a tightrope walker. The maneuver worked. She regained her balance and brought her breathing under control. Now all she'd have to worry about was tripping over the hem of her gown.

She gulped in air. Somewhere in her memory banks she remembered that stairs in medieval times were made uneven to slow down an enemy's advance if they breached the walls. The whole notion had seemed glamorous until now, when she'd almost broken her neck.

She refocused on navigating down the stairs. They should have installed handrails or running lights. Then she reminded herself that this tour company wouldn't be so foolish as to create a dangerous situation. If there was an accident, a law firm, like the one she worked for, would sue them out of existence.

Irene reached out for a wall to help guide her. The sudden movement caused her legs to get tangled in the fabric of her long gown. She twisted around, but that only made it worse. Her veil wound around her face. She screamed in frustration as she tried to peel it loose and lost her balance again.

Her feet landed on the lip of the next step with a

jolt. She slipped and pitched forward into the darkness. Flapping her arms like a crazed baby bird learning how to fly, her eyes squeezed shut. She was going to break every bone in her body.

Strong arms wrapped around her. "Don't worry," Logan said. "I've got you."

She clung to his neck as he gathered her closer. She could feel his heart beat against her chest, or was that hers? Random thoughts popped in and out. How had he reached her so fast? Did he think she was clumsy? Too heavy?

Pathetic. He'd saved her, and all she could think about was her weight. Still…

She squirmed in his arms. "Thank you, but you can put me down."

"And blow my one chance to rescue a beautiful damsel in distress? Not a chance. Besides, we're almost there."

Although the bagpipes were louder and she could hear the haunting notes of a flute, the mist was as dense as ever. "How can you tell?" she said.

She felt a rumble of laughter rise in his chest. "It's a guess. I haven't a clue."

Chapter Eight

At the bottom of the stairs, the mist thinned and the Highland melody drifted to an end. Whispered conversations filled the void left by the music. She had the sensation that she'd entered another world. Irene clung to Logan as they entered a wide, circular alcove.

Mist cleared, as though chased away by the torch lights that hung in brackets on stone walls. The double doors closed behind her and locked, which did nothing to calm her nerves. Standing in the clearing was Lady Roselyn and the other tour guests.

When her rescuer set her down, Irene's legs buckled, and Logan kept his arms around her a moment longer than seemed necessary before he released her. He shielded the diary from the group as he handed it to her. "You threw this when you tripped." He rubbed his neck and grinned. "It hit me in the head."

She grimaced. "Sorry, but thank you," she whispered as Lady Roselyn approached.

"Yes, thank you, Logan, for saving Irene," Lady Roselyn said. "First steps on this journey can be tricky if you're not careful." She turned toward the group. "Please stay close together as we proceed to our destination. It's easy to get lost, which is the reason we selected an entrance near our activities." She motioned for everyone to step in line behind her as the corridor narrowed. "As we proceed toward the Great Hall," she said, "feel free to look around. This is not one of those tours where you're instructed not to touch. Touching is part of the experience. Stirling Castle played a major role in the Scottish struggle for independence from England's rule. As a result, the castle was constantly under attack. To our left is a hallway that leads to the castle's Chapel Royal, where our weddings take place, and further down are housed the bedchambers for our guests. And here we are."

Lady Roselyn stepped aside, extending her arm to present the entrance to a banquet hall. Banners hung from the ceiling in alternating shades of reds and greens. "Welcome," she said dramatically, "to the thirteenth century."

There was a flurry of activity in the Great Hall. Men were bringing boughs indoors from pine, holly, and fir trees and placing them in piles, while women turned them into garlands and wreaths. Musicians warmed up their instruments, and an artist sketched a wolfhound puppy chewing on a bone. A fireplace large enough to roast a full-grown cow blazed happily on the far side of the room, and over the mantel were crossed swords and a shield so highly polished it shone like a mirror. The smell of baking bread laced with herbs danced in the air. The scene was equal parts overwhelming and thrilling.

Irene spun around. Everywhere she looked was a buzz of activity. Because of the detailed journal entries in her mother's diary, the setting before her felt like a scene from a well-loved book. Her mother's words had come to life. Irene pressed her arms against her waist to control her excitement, wishing her sister were here.

Lady Roselyn raised her voice to get everyone's

attention. "My sisters and I will each lead a group of you to your rooms. Bridget is in charge of escorting the men, and Fiona will escort Irene and Julia. I will escort Sean and Ann to their suite. We've stretched the rules a bit to make your accommodations as comfortable as possible. Although we have a full schedule and our time here is limited, we've learned that having private quarters where you can relax and get away from the new sights and sounds is a welcome opportunity and helps make your experiences all the more enjoyable."

"It is as I've always imagined," Ann said.

Stunned, Irene turned to look at her. Sean and Logan looked as shocked. For a brief moment, Ann seemed happy and engaged, and her eyes focused. But then, just as before, her animation didn't last. In the next moment she was leaning on her husband, Sean, as Lady Roselyn guided them down a corridor. Unfazed, Bridget motioned for the men to follow her in the opposite direction.

"Ann and Sean are truly a lovely couple," Fiona said to Irene and Julia. "We have great hopes for both of them. Are you ready?" Fiona's sunny expression was contagious. She'd changed from the modern clothes she'd worn at the ticket booth to a more century-appropriate gown. While Lady Roselyn wore blue, and Bridget a shade of forest green, Fiona's gown looked like it had captured the firelight, which brought out the red highlights in her blond hair. Like her sisters, Fiona wore a red-and-green tartan sash over one shoulder.

"Your rooms are not far away," Fiona said. "In this century, they are referred to as chambers. That reminds me. For our female guests, the bathrooms, or garderobes, as they are called in this century, are connected to your quarters. That said, and even though they were scrubbed and cleaned this morning, they are basically holes in the wood plank benches and empty into the streams below the castle." Fiona gave an apologetic shrug. "We've set a bowl of oranges stuffed with fragrant cloves nearby, as there might be an odor. Actually, count on a smell and be pleasantly surprised if there isn't one. Sorry. Oh, good, here we are. Irene, this is your chamber. Julia has the one further down the hallway."

Inside was a four-poster bed with vibrant red velvet curtains hanging from the top of the bed's square frame that cascaded like a crimson waterfall onto the wood floor. The bedspread was the same shade of velvet, its hem braided with alternating green and gold threads. The bed looked so inviting, Irene yawned in response, and caught Fiona smiling.

"For some reason our guests are tired when they first begin the tour," Fiona said. "Make yourself comfortable while I show Julia to her chamber. We gather for the first feast of the day after you've rested, and the meal will also include games my sisters and I have planned for our guests' entertainment. Would you like me to send someone to help you find your way back to the Great Hall? We've made quite a few twists and turns along the way."

Irene sat on the side of the bed. "No, thank you. I never get lost."

When the door shut, her room felt even more cozy and warm. A fire blazed opposite the bed, and a tapestry hung near a leaded-glass window. The tapestry was as welcome as the room. It pictured a meadow frosted with snow and a path that led to a cottage with the image of a Scottish thistle painted on the door. A wisp of smoke trailed from the cottage's chimney, and its windows glowed with warmth.

Irene yawned again. Maybe she'd take just a short nap.

Chapter Nine

An hour and a half later, Bridget checked on the guests. They were still asleep. At least something was going right. She raced into the Great Hall and slid to a stop on the polished floor just as her sister, Lady Roselyn, was finishing her speech.

Half listening, Bridget waited until her sister had finished. Those gathered were a handful of castle inhabitants who had direct contact with the guests, while many more who were not present acted as support. The matchmakers believed that everyone, from cook to knight to invited guest, should have the opportunity to be part of the magic. There were always variations on the speech, depending on the group, but over the years the theme hadn't changed. It always began with: "Put your troubles and worries aside, enjoy the adventure," and finished with, "Let love in."

Bridget remembered listening to her grandmother and mother as they made this speech. In those days, she had dreamed of the time when she and her sisters could step into the family tradition. Her grandmother and mother had made it look easy.

As Lady Roselyn finished and was answering questions, Bridget stepped forward and lowered her voice. "Can I speak with you privately?"

Lady Roselyn kept her smile in place. "Can't it wait?"

"We have uninvited guests."

To her sister's credit, Lady Roselyn's expression never wavered. The only indication that she understood the severity of their situation was a slight narrowing of her gaze. "How many?"

"Three."

"Are they…contained?"

Bridget gave a sharp nod. "Fiona has them under guard."

Lady Roselyn apologized to the group with a promise that she'd "Be right back."

Bridget motioned for her sister to follow her. That Lady Roselyn's farewell had been clipped as well as cliché had not escaped notice. A few of the staff exchanged glances or rolled their eyes before heading toward their assigned stations.

Bridget and her sister entered the chamber, behind the Great Hall, that the sisters used as their office. At first glance it resembled every other chamber in the castle. There was an oversized fireplace, period furniture, and rolls of parchment documents and maps, as well as books that had been handwritten and illuminated by nuns or monks. The tapestries that hung on the wall to chase out the damp and cold completed the illusion that this was a chamber like all the others in the castle.

Things were not always as they seemed.

The images on the tapestries weren't of pastoral scenes and people frolicking over meadows, or recreations of gruesome battles, they were of doors and gateways. Entrances to gardens, to Egyptian pyramids, to castles, to Asian and European palaces… From the ornate to the plain, the woven images of doors, so life-like in every detail, looked as though they could open.

When the sisters entered, Lady Roselyn walked calmly toward her desk. "I've decided you've overreacted. These people you and your sister have detained will turn out to be part of the castle's staff. We've all been working too hard. We need a vacation. Someplace warm."

Bridget understood her sister's reluctance. There was no room for mistakes. The slightest deviation had a domino effect. But facts were still facts. "If we get through unscathed, I'll hold you to your vacation speech. When the men were apprehended, Liam locked them in the dungeon."

"The dungeon?" Lady Roselyn's response came out in a squeak.

"We didn't have a choice." Bridget spread a tapestry aside, revealing an entrance to one of the passageways that crisscrossed behind the castle walls. Taking a torch from the wall, she descended the staircase.

"I don't like this place," Lady Roselyn said behind Bridget. "I think these passageways are haunted."

"There aren't any ghosts. Mother said she checked."

"We were children," Lady Roselyn said. "What was she supposed to say?"

A short time later, they reached the dungeon, which spread like a rabbit warren beneath the castle. Sword drawn, Fiona kept watch over an iron grate on the stone floor. The grate was placed in the ceiling of a large cell. Below, three men, dressed in costumes of the thirteenth century, feasted on pork roast, ham, and an assortment of breads and cheese.

"For the love of chocolate," Lady Roselyn said, "Fiona. Put away your weapon. I swear you grow more like our grandmother every day." Lady Roselyn peered closer. "I recognize those beady eyes. Those are the men who caused so much trouble in the café earlier today. I had them removed. How did they get back in here?"

Fiona set the sword on a wall bracket next to other medieval weapons. "They pretended to be part of the staff. It wasn't until they were here that someone noticed and reported them to Liam. We didn't know where else to put them."

"You've made them comfortable, at least. Can they see us?"

Fiona shook her head. "They've been quiet so far. Liam said they gave up without a fuss."

"Well, what's done is done. They'll just have to remain here until after the wedding on Christmas Eve."

"They'll want to sue us when this is all over," Bridget said.

"Tell them they will have to stand in line."

Chapter Ten

Irene awoke with a start and had that momentary, "Where am I?" feeling before she realized where she was. She slid off the bed and stretched. From the window, she noticed that it was already dusk, and the room, no, the chamber, Irene corrected, remembering the name Fiona had called it, was dimly lit. A cheery little fire did its best to chase away the chill air, and a bouquet of lavender stood on a table nearby. She couldn't remember the last time she'd taken a nap in the middle of the day, but she felt refreshed and looked forward to exploring the castle. She reached for the diary and headed out into the quiet hallway.

She hadn't really lied to Fiona about getting lost. She did have a unique system when she traveled, but it was more than that. The reason Irene wasn't worried about losing her way in Stirling Castle was because of her mother's diary.

Her mother had written with such detail about every nook, every alcove, and every chamber in Stirling Castle that Irene felt as though she had a personal road map of the area. There was even mention of hidden passageways, dungeons, and what passed for a library in the thirteenth century. Irene's stepfather, however, said the notion that his wife had visited Scotland was ridiculous. He was certain she'd never traveled outside the continental United States. Traveling to Europe had been a dream of theirs, but they'd never had the chance.

And yet Irene and her sister were convinced that their mother had been here before. That was the only explanation that made sense, which only added to the puzzle.

After a short time her good intentions to explore ended when she realized she was hungry. Exploring a castle on an empty stomach proved a distraction, especially when she could smell the rich aroma of fruit pies baking in the oven.

Irene gave up and followed the scent of cinnamon and nutmeg. It took longer than she expected, but she hoped she was getting close. Her mother's notations weren't as helpful as she'd thought they would be, and the photos in the brochures Irene had read on the plane had made the kitchens seem closer to the Great Hall than they apparently were. She'd misinterpreted the distance. Kitchens were fire hazards in this time period. Logically the best solution was to situate them as far from the living quarters as was practical. She'd read that some kitchens were even located in an outside building.

She paused. "Of course." Changing directions, she raced down the ground floor corridor where the baking smells had been the strongest. She'd dismissed the area, as it looked like it led into the courtyard.

A few minutes later she reached a dead end. There was a flurry of activity and a parade of people coming and going, carrying baskets of fruit, sacks of flour, and spices. Irene entered the kitchens and was immediately engulfed in the sights, smells, and sounds of baking bread, baked apples, and laughter. The compact room was filled with women bent to their tasks. Some peeled and sliced apples, some kneaded and braided dough into loaves of bread, while others washed dishes or wiped down counters. Bridget was in the center of the activity.

Bridget had filled tins with sliced apples, sprinkled nutmeg and cinnamon, then placed rolled-out dough on top. She decorated each with sections of dough cut out in the shape of apples and leaves. Her creations were a work of art.

Irene paused, not sure if she was allowed entrance. One of the women nudged Bridget, who looked up, her expression hesitant at first but then melting into a smile.

"You found us," she said.

"Such yummy smells. I couldn't resist."

Bridget laughed, the sound so natural it brought an answering smile to Irene's face. "The pastries in this country are an adventure for the tongue, my mother would say. The French say the English food is too plain, and for the most part I agree. The French have mastered many things, including perfecting anything to do with chocolate, but I love the simplicity of a good fruit pie and a well-baked bread. The pies have almost cooled. Sit a while, and I'll get you a slice."

"Do you cook pheasants in your pies?" Irene said, remembering one of the notations in the guide books.

"You know your history. The answer is a resounding no. We try to cook authentic recipes for the time, but there are some I have refused, and that is at the top of the list."

Irene noticed a saying painted on the wall, titled *A Recipe For A Successful Match*:

Begin with a mixture of friendship,
Communication and respect.

Add a dash of attraction.
Blend equal parts of commitment,
Trust, and honesty.
Now fold in a generous cup of love.

"That is a beautiful saying," Irene said.

"It's been in our family for generations." Bridget cut a generous slice of pie, set it onto a plate, and handed it to Irene. "The poem also serves as the matchmaker motto."

Irene took a bite of pie and closed her eyes as the combination of flavors melted in her mouth. "This is delicious," she said with her mouth full. She swallowed and cut into the pie for another bite. "What you do is a family business, then?"

"It's more of a calling."

One of the women whispered in Bridget's ear. Bridget's expression changed as though a cloud had passed over the sun. She took off her apron and hung it on a hook. "I have to go, but stay, finish your pie. Mary will take good care of you and make sure you get back to your room, or you can participate in the games going on in the Great Hall."

"I'm not much on games." Irene rose. "Can I help?"

Bridget hesitated at the door. "Thank you for asking, but Fiona said she has things under control."

Chapter Eleven

Irene had declined both a second slice of pie and Mary's help to show her the way back. She wanted to make sure she had time to explore the castle before the feast. And the library seemed like the perfect place to start, as her mother had mentioned it more than once. Maybe she'd find the answers there. When Irene had first read the entries, she had supposed her mother had done extensive research. Except there were huge discrepancies between some of her mother's accounts and the reference books she'd read on the flight. Her mother said there were hundreds of portraits at Stirling Castle. The reference materials claimed portraits were seldom housed there because the castle was always changing hands or under siege.

The reference books also mentioned that in the sixteenth century King James V had ordered the construction of more windows and shallow niches to house statues of Greek and Roman gods. The guide books said these statues had survived the wars and were on the "must see" list for anyone visiting the castle, but Irene hadn't seen anything of them. The sisters did stress they'd recreated a thirteenth-century experience, so King James V wouldn't have been around for another two or three hundred years. Had the sisters managed to cloak the statues somehow?

Irene smiled to herself, impressed by their attention

to detail. And people said *she* was a stickler for facts.

She checked a small diagram in the diary, drawn in her mother's hand. According to the map, the library was at the end of the next bend in the corridor. The hallways in the castle were like an elaborate maze lined with portraits of nobles and their children, and this one was no exception. No wonder Fiona had thought Irene might get lost. Without her mother's diary, there was a pretty good chance she would have. The corridor came to an abrupt dead end, and on Irene's right was an arched doorway.

Flanking the entrance stood life-size statues of knights in full suits of chainmail, complete with helmets and golden spurs. Inside the library, the walls were lined with shelves stuffed with scrolls and books. A fire burned in the hearth, and in the center of the room in a place of honor lay an illuminated manuscript.

She approached it reverently, as though she'd entered a place of worship. The manuscript was a work of art. Wide margins were filled with intricate designs of rabbits, birds, and stylized flowers. The illuminations were so vibrant they seemed to give off their own light.

Irene held her fingers over the pages. They begged to be touched, but even the thought felt sacrilegious.

"The book is meant to be read."

Irene snapped her hand back, like a child caught with her hand in the cookie jar. "Who's there?"

Logan emerged from a corner by a small window, looking even taller than she remembered. Were his eyes always that blue? He held up a leather-bound book as though to show he came in peace. "I didn't mean to startle you. I was on a quest."

She also registered that his tunic was forest green

with gold piping. The same colors were also used in her bedchamber. Now, why did she make that comparison? She shook her head as though to clear her thoughts. "Aren't you interested in the games going on in the Great Hall?"

He shrugged with a smile. "Too many people. What's your excuse?"

"I don't like games," she admitted. "You mentioned a quest?"

He motioned to the book he held. "I was looking for the poem *Beowulf* and got distracted when I found this one written by Sun Tzu, titled *The Art of War*. One of my favorite quotes by him is 'If you know the enemy and know yourself, you need not fear the result of a hundred battles.' "

Irene nodded, leaning over to examine the book he held. "That is a beautiful saying, but speaking personally, following its advice to know yourself would be the tricky part." She glanced up at him. "This book is in Chinese. Can you read the language?"

"My mother had both a translated copy as well as one in Chinese. I recognized the symbols on the cover. She loved the idea of reading books in their original language." He paused, replacing the book on the shelf. "She doesn't read much anymore."

Irene felt a wave of pain emanate from him when he spoke about his mother. "Your mother sounds amazing."

He cleared his throat. "Back to *Beowulf*. I haven't found it yet, but I'm not giving up."

She recognized that he didn't want to talk about his mother, and she understood completely. When mother was diagnosed with cancer, the last thing Irene and her sister had wanted was to see that look of pity in a person's eyes when they offered comfort.

Irene moved along the shelves filled with books interspersed with scrolls secured by wax seals. "*Beowulf* was the first book I read in grammar school that wasn't on the class assigned reading list," she said. "When I was a child, I loved that it was a story about castles, betrayals, warriors, battles, and a monster named Grendel, but I admit I really wanted more romance."

"*Beowulf* isn't what a child normally reads in grammar school. He's a completed hero, someone who fights against impossible odds. I'm impressed. What do you know—you have a nerd flag. You just don't fly it as boldly as the rest of us."

She reflected his smile. "Guilty as charged."

He tucked his book under his arm and selected a thin volume, thumbed through it, and then set it back on the shelf with a wink. "My theory is that Grendel is not only a misunderstood monster but that the sixth-century story is based on real historical events. A recent site in Denmark uncovered a hall where the story might actually have taken place. I'm looking to see if they have any information in the library. I figured since I had time on my hands it was worth exploring."

She liked that he was drawn to those who fought even though the odds weren't stacked in their favor. "Any luck?"

He seemed distracted and replaced the book he'd been holding back on the shelf. "Not yet, but I enjoy a good hunt."

"You sound like an archeologist…"

"We can't reveal our jobs, remember? Your turn.

What are you searching for?"

"Is it that obvious?" She shook her head, avoiding his gaze, and pulled one of the scrolls out of its cubby. She could pretend to read it, but it was written in Latin. She put it back. She didn't know how much she wanted to share. The one time she had, she'd received a lecture on why would a mother lie to her daughters and husband about traveling to Scotland and then bequeath them a diary that not only claimed the opposite but suggested an affair with a mystery man named Connor? The lecture was followed by a theory suggesting her mother had made the whole thing up.

"Maybe I simply wanted to get away for a while," she offered.

"A quest seeker always recognizes his own kind."

Irene rarely had shared the mysteries she'd discovered in her mother's diary. Chad, her ex, had suggested she was obsessed with learning about her mother and insisted she seek professional help or meds. Maybe both. His lack of understanding had highlighted the gulf between them. He had also harbored the delusion that cheating was okay.

Chad had tried to make the argument that seeing other people would make their relationship stronger. He said she should be honored he'd chosen her best friend, Silvia, instead of a random woman. Irene had to give him credit for one thing. Nothing ruffled the jerk. He'd made his argument with his best courtroom charm, moments after Irene had discovered the two of them together. Irene believed in being faithful to the one you professed to love. Her ex obviously did not.

But she barely knew Logan. So if he thought she was nuts about the mysteries in her mother's diary, it wouldn't matter. After tomorrow she'd never see him again. Besides, he might be able to help.

She took a deep breath and produced her mother's diary. "You're right. I am on a quest of my own. More like a journey to unravel a mystery. I'm trying to understand my mother's interest in Stirling Castle and why she not only kept her time here a secret but also wanted my twin sister and me to visit." She handed the diary to Logan and opened it to a page with an illustration of the library. "My mother wrote in her diary about her time here, including detailed maps of the interior of the castle."

Logan sat on the edge of a table and examined the page. "These drawings are amazing. This is the book you dropped on the stairs."

She nodded. "You're very observant."

He flipped over to the next page and then back again. "It comes in handy in my line of work. I gather the diary is the real reason you're on this tour. You're not looking for a quickie romance with one of the men in kilts. My guess is that you are more the happily-ever-after type."

She turned away and pretended to study another bank of scrolls. If he could see that about her so easily, why hadn't her ex? "What about you?"

"Don't you think I'm looking for a wife?"

His question was playful, almost teasing, except the expression in his eyes was serious and held her gaze. It made her wonder. Was he the real deal? She'd gone down this path before on first dates, hoping for the best only to be disappointed. "Julia's available," she said, knowing her remark was a test.

"Not my type." His response was so quick it took

her by surprise. In a very good way.

"What is your type?" She wished she could pull her question back. What was she thinking? More importantly, why did it matter?

"My type?" His grin widened. "No one's asked me that question in a long time. But since you asked…I'm looking for someone who's scary-smart and not afraid to dress up as Wonder Woman."

A delightful shiver, like raw silk over bare skin, brushed over her. She moved away from the shelves toward the fireplace, in the hopes he wouldn't notice the heat of a blush rising on her face. She had a vintage collection of Wonder Woman comics. "I would think you could find plenty of candidates who fit your description, at a comic book convention."

He slid down from the desk and joined her by the fire. "Not as many as you'd think. I have a third item that is my deal breaker."

The chamber warmed as the fire glowed a little brighter. "What is it?"

His smile was mischievous. "We don't know each other well enough yet. Let's get to work on your puzzle. Do you mind if I look at more of the illustrations and maps in your mother's diary? I'm a pretty good detective."

She seized on the distraction of trying to find out his occupation. "You're a policeman."

Logan laughed as he opened it and started turning the pages. "First I'm an archeologist and now I'm a policeman."

"Back at the café, Bridget mentioned she thought you were a rugby player."

He laughed in earnest, a trait that seemed natural

for him. "Remember, we're not to tell each other our occupations. Out of curiosity, what profession would be a deal breaker for you?"

"I could ask you the same question."

"Fair enough. Maybe the sisters have a point. Sometimes a person's job doesn't reflect who they are." He paused over a photograph taped to one of the pages. "This is you as a small child, maybe seven or eight. I recognize the smile. All teeth and bright eyes, like you're about to burst into a belly laugh."

"Hey," she said, nudging him in the ribs.

He leaned in. "It was a compliment. The woman in the middle looks familiar."

"That's my mother, and there's always been a strong family resemblance. My sister, Louise, is the one on the other side. We're twins, but we don't look anything alike. My mother was also named Irene. It was a tradition in her family that the first daughter born would be named Irene, and the second, Louise." Irene felt the familiar catch in her throat. She pressed her lips together for a brief moment before she spoke. "The picture was taken long before she became ill and passed away."

Logan lifted his gaze from the photograph. "I'm sorry."

She nodded a thank you, but she wasn't ready to share the details of the last days of the illness that had taken her mother away too soon.

Logan refocused his attention on the photograph. "It's more than a family resemblance. I saw a portrait of a woman who looks a lot like your mother on one of the walls leading toward the library. I remember because she was wearing earrings that look like your pendant.

Maybe you and your sister have Scottish ancestry?"

Irene shivered as though someone had opened a window and let in a cold blast of air. She rubbed her arms, but the sensation remained. Like most people these days, she and her sister wondered where their ancestors had come from. Louise had once asked their mother about the possibility of a Scottish heritage. Her mother's answer had been a resounding no, and she had changed the subject. Looking back, Irene thought their mother's overreaction seemed odd. If there was a connection to Scotland, why did her mother want to keep it a secret?

Chapter Twelve

The door to the library banged open, interrupting Irene's thoughts.

A man rushed in, his mop of dark hair flopping over his angular face. Irene recognized him as one of the men who had come with them on the tour. "Lady Roselyn and her sisters are going nuts looking for you two," he said, out of breath. "The feast is about to begin. I stalled for as long as I could, but I swear the youngest sister, Fiona, could charm the spots off my Dalmatian puppy. Before I knew what was happening, I had volunteered to find you."

"Thanks, Grant," Logan said, reaching for Irene's hand.

She pulled back, slipping her hand free. After Logan's mention of a portrait likeness of her mother, a feast was the farthest thing from her mind. "Can you show me where you found the portrait?"

He held her gaze for a brief moment, then nodded.

Grant turned his saucer-wide eyes from Irene to Logan and back again. "Hey, guys, we don't have time."

Logan ignored Grant and turned his attention to Irene as though the man were invisible. "The portrait is hanging along one of the corridors. You may have passed it on your way here. I'm surprised you didn't notice it. The resemblance is uncanny."

Irene held the diary against her chest with both hands. She was struggling with the same question. "My mother never mentioned any connection to Scotland. It's probably just a good likeness. I've heard that we all have at least one lookalike in the world."

"They're called doppelgangers. But the woman was wearing earrings similar to your pendant. That's what really caught my attention. I planned to find you, but then I discovered the library." He grinned. "Short attention span. I kept getting distracted at school. My black lab and I were a lot alike. We'd be playing ball together, and he'd see a squirrel and be off on an adventure, and I'd be right behind him. My mother would say it was because I had an active mind. My teachers had a different name for it."

Irene fingered the snowflake pendant, thinking their mothers were a lot alike. She also sensed he was trying to lighten her mood. "I used to get into trouble for daydreaming in class. My mother defended me to the teacher and said it was because the course work was boring."

He nodded his head toward the picture in the diary. "What do you think? Do you want to skip the feast and find the portrait?"

Grant cut in between them. "Seriously. We have to leave. Now. And skipping is not an option. Something about rules and their sending out guards if I didn't bring you back."

Logan looked as though he was having trouble trying not to smile. "Grant looks like he'll have a coronary if we don't follow him. Would it be all right if we went to see it after the feast?"

Chapter Thirteen

She hadn't answered his question. Was Logan right? Could her family have Scottish heritage? That would explain her mother's interest. In a fog, Irene had followed Logan and Grant back to the Great Hall. Why hadn't she insisted they find the portrait? They'd made so many twists and turns that, by the time they arrived, Irene felt dizzy and disoriented, the complete opposite of her professional persona of a cool, calm, and always-in-control prosecutor. She felt like she was standing on a cliff, afraid to look down. The drop could be inches or miles. One she'd survive, the other…

Lady Roselyn raised her voice to announce dinner was served and led the group to a long trestle table dressed for a feast. Handwritten place cards, each with a person's name scrolled in a flourish of Old English-style script, took the guesswork out of where to sit. The Great Hall had been transformed into a winter wonderland of tree branches and candlelight. Irene's practical side screamed "fire hazard" while the softer side of her gave an audible sigh. She half expected to see butterfly-size fairies dancing around the tree limbs.

She found her seat and picked up the place card. On the eve of her sister's wedding, she and Louise had snuck into the reception room and thrown away all the place cards. By then, their mother had been in decline, and Louise's mother-in-law had taken over all the wedding preparations. In addition to the arranged seating, the woman had ordered that the tables be set up in rounds to accommodate no more than four people each. She insisted the guests didn't want to mingle with anyone they didn't already know. Louise held an opposite opinion.

Irene's sister had used what they did as a test for her future husband, and he'd passed with flying colors. When he realized what had happened, he gathered his friends and, with the help of the staff, brought in larger tables.

Irene never knew what her sister's husband said to his mother that day, but from that moment on, she'd welcomed Louise more as a daughter then someone who was in competition for her son's affections.

This small rebellion had turned a solemn, stodgy wedding into a real celebration of family and friends. Irene fingered the place card before setting it back on the table. Louise had always been the one who leapt without a net. The only reason Irene was here was because Louise's child was due soon. Her mother always said things happened for a reason, even if they couldn't be understood at the time.

Lady Roselyn took her position at the head of the table and indicated for everyone to find their chairs. Directly to her right was a place card for Ann, one for Sean, then for Logan, and finally Julia's at the end. On Lady Roselyn's left were place cards for people Irene hadn't met yet. Caitlin, the laird's daughter, who would be getting married at midnight, according to what the tour group had been told, and Angus, a man who looked like everyone's dream of a knight-in-shining armor. Next to them were place cards for Grant, Irene, and someone named Sam.

There was a brief period of confusion while everyone found their chairs, and then a quiet lull descended over the group. With Irene the only exception, everyone was seated beside someone they already knew, so there was no reason to strike up a conversation. Was that what her sister had suspected would happen when she'd learned about the arranged seating? Being organized wasn't a bad thing, but in certain circumstances it could rob an event of its spontaneity and discovery.

Irene placed both hands on the high-backed chair and kept that in mind as she tried to ignore the hemmed-in feeling. Lady Roselyn had placed her between Grant and a complete stranger.

"Hello, gorgeous," a man said as he pulled out her chair. "My name is Sam."

She jerked a nod and scooted her chair in close to the table. He seemed like a perfectly nice man. He had that five-day-old beard thing going for him that some women found sexy. On some guys it worked, but on Sam all she could think of was that he was too lazy to shave.

She jumped.

Sam's hand was on her knee. His fingers squeezed as he slid her a sideways glance. She wrenched it away. "Not cool, Sam."

He tucked in his chin and pouted. "We were seated next to each other. I thought the sisters meant…" He took a drink from his apple cider, made a face, and motioned to one of the servers for something stronger.

"Sam was out of line," Grant said, leaning toward her. "I'll talk to him. We're both trying to figure out the rules. Julia and I and a lot of our friends attend Renaissance and medieval faires. The matchmaker's ad was irresistible. *Tired of failed relationships? Take a journey back in time and find your match,* it said. I liked everything about the pitch. Since the three of us love going to these types of festivals, we felt it was a good fit. Besides, Julia's been here before, and she wanted to return." He stole a glance toward Julia. Even the casual observer could sense the attraction he felt for her. Grant ducked his head and fingered his goblet. "The tour is not what I…that is…"

"May I have your attention?" Lady Roselyn said, raising her voice above the music. "All the food is authentic to the thirteenth century. For those of you with food allergies, we've taken our selections into consideration. Everything presented here tonight is perfectly safe to eat. Enjoy." She then motioned for the servers to start the procession.

Each course was presented with much fanfare and description. The first course was a thin broth with bacon, followed by pigeon stuffed with herbs, in currant sauce. There was stewed hare, except Irene couldn't banish the image of cute bunny rabbits, so she declined. When the eel in a spicy mustard sauce was presented, Logan made a gagging sound. Irene smiled, choked on a turnip, and covered her mouth with her linen napkin to smother a laugh.

Lady Roselyn stood once more and clinked her goblet with a knife to get everyone's attention. "I'd like to make an announcement. The desserts will be presented in a few moments, and more will be offered during the wedding feast, but now I'd like to introduce our wedding couple, Caitlin and her groom-to-be,

Angus."

Everyone at the table clapped—everyone, that was, except Julia. She sat as still as a statue carved from a solid piece of cold marble. She dropped her knife on her plate and overturned her goblet in her haste to leave.

Stunned silence gripped those at the table for a moment, and then everyone started talking at once. Angus rose to go after Julia, but Caitlin held him back with a touch of her hand on his arm. He hesitated before he pulled away and left in the direction Julia had run. Irene had witnessed the instant recognition between Angus and Julia. They knew each other, and the announcement that Caitlin and Angus were to be married had been a shock to Julia.

Irene knew how it felt to be caught off guard. Catching her ex with another woman had been bad enough: learning he thought she should understand and just "get over it" had caused her to go into a mini meltdown. Fortunately, she'd had her sister to bring things back into perspective. Louise had reminded Irene that it was a good thing she'd learned what a creep he was *before* they got married.

Irene wondered who was there for Julia. Angus had chased after her, but was he really the one Julia should be talking to right now? Maybe she should stay out of it. After all, she didn't know Julia that well, and this was obviously some sort of love triangle. Or maybe it was part of the entertainment of the tour experience? Except it seemed too real. She could tell heartache when she saw it. Caitlin was sobbing, and Lady Roselyn was trying unsuccessfully to comfort her.

Grant and Sam were talking in whispers across

Irene, and on the other side of the table Logan and his father were trying to calm Ann. She kept alternating between attempting to leave and glancing toward Irene. Her gaze was focused and her expression intense as she ignored both her son and her husband. Irene had the distinct impression that Ann was trying to say something to her.

Irene focused on Ann.

The response was instant as Ann responded and mouthed the words: *Go after Julia.*

Irene sprang to her feet.

Chapter Fourteen

Irene raced after Julia down a long corridor, but the sounds of angry voices stopped her short. She peered around the corner. In an alcove, Angus and Julia were engaged in a heated argument. He shook his head and stepped back, then spun around and ran in the opposite direction from the Great Hall.

Julia sank to the ground like a rag doll.

Irene rushed over, kneeling beside her. "Julia…"

"Men are pigs."

Irene reached for Julia's hand. She definitely looked like a woman who'd had her heart stomped on. "What did he say to you?"

"Angus said that he is in love with Caitlin," Julia said, gulping air. "In fact, he admitted that when we first met he was only interested in me because Caitlin had rejected him. I was the rebound girl." Julia swiped at her tearstained face with the back of her hand and ground her teeth together. "The worst part was that I think I knew it all along and was so desperate I ignored the warning signs. He had the attention span of a two-year-old in a candy shop and kept forgetting my name. There were zero sparks coming from him, which was confusing. He was gorgeous, and everything I thought I wanted, so naturally I made up excuses for him."

Irene put her arm around Julia, and the woman slumped against her, sobbing into her shoulder. "You're going to have to catch me up to speed." She stroked Julia's arm in the same way her sister had when Irene first learned of her fiancé's betrayal. Having a friend to talk to that day had made all the difference.

"Angus and I met the first time I was here," Julia said between sobs. "I liked the idea that he was actually from the thirteenth century and a real knight. He was all my fantasies come true. He was chivalrous, handsome…"

"Wait. You mean he acted like a knight from the medieval ages, right? Not that he was actually from that time period."

Julia sniffled, wiping her eyes again with the heel of her hand. "No, Angus *is* from the thirteenth century."

Irene started to say that was impossible, then changed her mind. She remembered how patient her sister had been as Irene was freaking out after she'd caught her ex with her best friend. Louise had listened patiently, and then announced that they were leaving Seattle for the weekend. Irene didn't bother to protest. She'd learned early that, even though Louise was younger by two minutes and three seconds, saying no to Louise was not an option when she was in protective mode.

They'd spent the weekend in Vancouver, British Columbia, cried buckets of tears together, attended plays, eaten mounds of chocolate, and gone for long walks. At the end of the weekend, her ex and best friend's betrayal stung less, with the unexpected bonus that she and her sister had grown closer together.

And just as Louise had let Irene talk out her pain, Irene listened to Julia. Now was not the time to challenge Julia. She was too fragile. Irene smoothed hair back from Julia's face. "Angus does make a handsome knight. I can understand how he could have swept you off your feet."

Julia sniffed again. "You don't believe that he's from the thirteenth century. I didn't at first, either. When Angus and I met, I thought I'd found my soulmate, and even as starry-eyed as I was, I didn't take him at his word. But there are things about this castle and its inhabitants that don't make sense in any other way. I was caught up in the romance that we'd time traveled back to the thirteenth century."

"Julia, time travel is not…"

"Anything is possible. This world is like the one in *Brigadoon*. Angus told me that if two people loved each other enough, they can stay here together…as in forever. But something held me back, and I know now it was because I didn't really love him, and he certainly didn't love me. I used the excuse that I couldn't give up my life in the twenty-first century. I have a job I love and friends I care about. I told him that if he came with me, I'd help find a job for him, but he said if he left Stirling Castle the enchantment would be broken and everyone would die. Like an idiot, I came back to tell him I'd give up my life in the twenty-first century to be with him. But the first time I've seen him since coming back was at the dinner. That's when I learned he and Caitlin are getting married."

Irene rubbed both temples, trying to stem the tide of a building headache. She certainly understood the shock of betrayal and how it could turn a clear-thinking person's thoughts into a rollercoaster ride of wild imaginings. But time travel? "You're upset. I get that. And the story Angus told you is consistent with the plotline of *Brigadoon*. But you can't believe it's true."

Julia balled her fingers into fists. "Look around you, Dorothy: we're not in Kansas anymore. We really are in the thirteenth century."

"Ah, huh," Irene said, smoothing tear-dampened hair off Julia's cheek. "This has been a long day, and you received a big shock when you learned Angus was getting married. Why don't you let me help you to your room?"

Julia shrugged away. "You don't have to believe me. Ask the sisters. They can tell you all about the…"

A loud clang followed by a colorful string of oaths interrupted whatever else Julia had been about to say.

Julia glanced in the direction of the sound as a shadow of a smile brought color back into her face. "It's Grant. He's having trouble with the sword and sheath they provided with his costume. He has the same problem whenever we attend the Camlann Medieval faires in Washington State. He prefers a bow and a quiver of arrows."

Irene's thoughts reeled. There was no doubt in her mind that Julia believed Angus' fairy-tale explanation. Irene felt like she was on a runaway train with no end in sight. But at the end of the day, was there really any harm in believing in a fantasy for a few hours? At the stroke of midnight, like Cinderella and her pumpkin coach, things would be back to normal.

Grant walked toward them, still mumbling under his breath. Somehow the sheath and sword attached to his belt had twisted around behind him. "Bloody, soul-sucking…" Grant clapped his mouth shut and gave a slight flourish of greeting that seemed right in character for a knight. "Very sorry. I didn't see you. Laughable, I know. A warrior who can't handle a sword. Logan took to it right away."

Julia's eyes crinkled at the corners as Grant helped her to her feet. "You're a skilled archer," she said. "They should have given you a bow."

"Not as glamorous, though." His jaw tightened. "Are you all right? Angus is a fool."

Silence shimmered between Julia and Grant like moonlight on a mirror-smooth pond. Irene felt as though she were attending a play and this was the part right before the best friends discovered they loved each other. These two were locked in their own world of discovery.

"Julia," Irene said, "Is there anything more I can do?"

Julia gave a slight shake of her head.

Irene backed away, pointing over her shoulder in the direction of the Great Hall. "I think I'm going back before they send out a search party. These sisters are like mother hens. They want to know where everyone is at all times."

Both Julia and Grant nodded as they moved slowly and purposefully toward one another.

Chapter Fifteen

Logan stood at the open window. Clouds had moved in and blocked out the moon and stars. A light flickered in the distance, but otherwise it was pitch black. Even though the night was calm, he couldn't shake his unease. It must be his detective training. There were things about this place that didn't add up. For one, he'd never seen a reenactment this accurate. When he was a professional rugby player, before he'd blown out his knee for the third time, he'd stayed in the city of Stirling. Never once had he heard about this tour.

He wasn't having second thoughts about bringing his parents here for Christmas. His mother was in the mid-stages of Alzheimer's, and there had been signs that things were about to change for the worse. So when, out of the blue, she'd suggested this trip and particularly this tour, he and his dad had booked train tickets that same afternoon.

Now, with each hour that passed, his mother seemed to improve, which had him tipped upside down. There were moments of clarity, like when she had told him Irene's name, or argued that she wanted to help Julia, or just a few minutes ago discussed the meal she'd had on the train to Stirling. He shook his head in frustration. He couldn't remember what he'd eaten. How had she?

"May I join you?"

Logan would have recognized that voice anywhere. He knew he was grinning like a kid at a comic book convention, but he couldn't help it. Irene had that effect on him. He nodded and made room for her by the window. "How is Julia?"

"Actually, I think she's going to be fine. Grant is with her. Did you know they are friends?"

"Makes sense. Julia was all he talked about when we were getting ready. I thought he'd trip over his tongue when he first saw her in that red dress."

Irene smiled. "Well, I think Julia is starting to realize she likes him, as well. How's your mother?"

He liked that Irene had asked. Most women had other topics on their agenda, like which car they wanted him to pick them up in, or what he was giving them for their birthday.

Thinking about where his mother was right now broadened his smile. "Lady Roselyn said that with Caitlin thinking of ways to turn her ex-fiancé into a live pincushion, it would be a good time for a break. She gave everyone assignments. My father is helping out in the kitchens. He's the chef in the family and jumped at the chance. Caitlin was too much of a mess to do anything, so Bridget took her under her wing. Lady Roselyn said she had the perfect distraction for my mother. Something about tapestries, needlepoint, and looms. My attention wandered when she started discussing how the colors in the yarn were made and how many types of stitches there were. Thankfully she gave me guard duty, but it's so quiet all I hear are crickets."

Irene leaned against the stone windowsill. The

breeze coming through the open window caressed her hair, easing it away from her face. "I ran into Lady Roselyn for a few minutes when I was leaving Julia, and she asked me if I wanted to join them. Learning how to make tapestries is one of those things that sounds cool, like knitting sweaters or weaving a blanket, but my sewing skills are abysmal. When I lose a button on a blouse, if I can't keep it closed with a safety pin or duct tape, I buy a new one. Very sad."

He smiled at her joke. He couldn't stop staring. Her profile was outlined in torchlight. He'd never seen anyone more lovely. She was all soft and pastel around the edges, with a strong inner core. He'd noticed that confidence at the café. If he hadn't stepped in to confront the trio of idiots harassing Bridget, he knew Irene had been poised to intervene. That was when he first really noticed her. She hadn't cared that she would have been outnumbered. All that mattered was that someone needed help.

"I'm glad you didn't go with them." His words hung in the air briefly before being swept away by the breeze. "Are you cold?" he said.

She shook her head and studied her hands as they rested on the ledge. "I'm glad I'm here with you. And I'm having fun on the tour. That's unexpected."

"I'm as surprised as you. Shocked, in fact. My mother always wanted to go to Scotland, and when her doctors told us that..." He paused for a deep breath before he continued. "Well, this seemed like the perfect time. If you don't mind my asking, why are you here on Christmas Eve?"

"You mean alone, without a family?" She seemed to be wrestling with a decision. When her expression lightened, he sensed she was beginning to trust him. "My mother died on Christmas Eve, and I'm trying to find out why this castle was so important to her."

Chapter Sixteen

Logan had slipped his hand in hers. It enveloped her with warmth. For all his strength, he didn't seem threatening. She wondered if anyone had ever given him the name Gentle Giant.

She was no petite, delicate flower herself. She'd played volleyball in high school and college and had continued on a recreation team for the law firm. Most men were intimidated by her height, which her mother had always believed was a good thing. Her mother also preached that insecure men were high maintenance and should be avoided at all cost. Irene should have taken her advice.

"I should probably check on my mother," Logan said.

She liked that he cared enough to want to look after Ann. Irene leaned a little closer to him as they moved down a corridor.

"You no doubt guessed," he continued, "my mother has Alzheimer's." He winced. "I wish you could have known her before she became ill."

"Tell me about her."

"Where to begin? She was a history teacher. I think that's the reason she wanted to come here. She loves everything medieval."

Irene thought about sharing that her mother and his had a lot in common, but paused when she noticed

Logan's mother in a well-lit room. He'd noticed her, as well, and stood beside the doorway.

Candlelight illuminated every corner of the room. A fireplace added more light as well as warmth. In the center of the room, Logan's mother was operating a loom under Lady Roselyn's watchful care. Yarn flew under Ann's skillful hands, and the patterns and colors created were stunning. But it wasn't the skill that took Irene by surprise: it was the expression on Ann's face.

She was laughing and chatting with Lady Roselyn as though they were old friends, and she looked a good ten to fifteen years younger. There was a glow about her that was hard to miss.

"Mother?" Logan said, entering the room as though he were walking on eggshells.

Ann's smile grew even more radiant as she turned toward him. "Son, you've grown so tall."

"Ann looks amazing," Irene said to Lady Roselyn.

Lady Roselyn's smile was unguarded and lit up her expression. Still smiling, she turned toward Irene. "Stirling Castle can have that effect on our guests. We'll leave mother and son alone while they catch up. Come. We're expected in the Great Hall."

Chapter Seventeen

Candles and firelight transformed the Great Hall into a scene out of a fairyland. Irene had never seen so much mistletoe in one place before. It hung from the ceiling and was draped like garlands over the high-backed chairs and windowsills. A carved Yule log candle held a place of honor in the center of a long trestle table. Logan had stayed behind to be with his mother, but everyone else had taken the assigned seats again.

"Let the games begin," Lady Roselyn announced. "My sisters and I have chosen our first participant at random. Bridget, our official entertainment coordinator, and Fiona, who is our romance specialist, have developed a new spin on a popular old game, Blind Man's Bluff. Since Fiona is busy with the wedding preparations, Bridget will explain the new rules."

Bridget stood and surveyed the crowd as though gauging how they might react. "In the original version of Blind Man's Bluff, a person is blindfolded and surrounded by other participants. He or she must then capture another player and correctly identify them. Because we are matchmakers, we have created our own version. The game starts out the same, but instead of trying to capture the others, the blindfolded person will kiss them. And here is the twist. When the kiss ignites a spark and is returned, the game ends." She winked. "Or, as we like to believe, the real story begins. The heart finds its true love when least expected. Shall we start?"

"Who is the lucky person?" Sam asked.

Lady Roselyn picked up a long, narrow silk cloth. "Irene, of course."

The banquet table was quickly cleared and moved against the wall to make room for the sisters' game. Everyone seemed to think Bridget's version sounded like a great idea. Everyone, that is, except Irene.

"They can't be serious," Irene said under her breath to Julia.

Julia stood beside her, a wide grin on her face. "They are very serious. You don't have to play if you don't want to, but it's fun. I promise."

"Kissing strangers?" Irene shuddered. "Isn't that a little, oh, I don't know…weird?"

Julia lifted her shoulders and grinned. "I think it could be exciting. Besides, the sisters try not to allow any creeps on the tour. You saw what happened with the three Neanderthals in the café earlier. I heard that after Logan confronted them in the café, the sisters sent them away. Lady Roselyn also noticed your reaction to Sam, so that's the reason he won't be participating in the game. So I don't understand your concern."

"Still, kissing a stranger… Is this how you and Angus met?"

"I wish. Unfortunately, no. Maybe if we had I wouldn't have made such a big mistake. I think I was in love with the idea of what Angus represented. Macho, drop-dead yummy-looking. But when we kissed there wasn't a spark. I thought that was because there was something wrong with me, and that sparks would develop over time. Boy, was I wrong. All that developed over time was that I blew what I thought we had out of proportion."

"What about Grant? Any sparks?"

Julia blushed a lovely shade of rosy-pink. "Fireworks on steroids. I think that's the real reason the matchmaker sisters allowed me on this tour. They knew there was someone for me, but it just wasn't Angus." Julia pulled Irene to her feet. "Now, stop stalling. You don't have to have any big lip-locks, and you get to determine how long you kiss. A peck on the lips, at most, and you can be on to the next person. You can also stop at any time. Think of it this way: They always say you have to kiss a lot of frogs before you find your prince."

Chapter Eighteen

Irene really wished Julia would have used another comparison rather than frogs. Irene couldn't get the image of the cold, disgusting, slimy creatures out of her mind. Yes, she'd definitely kissed her share. She shuddered, as the blindfold was tied in place, and tried to stay calm as she was turned around and around in the center of the Great Hall. The first few turns, she kept count. After that, she gave over to the experience. When she was brought to a stop, she felt disoriented, which of course was the point, but her sense of hearing and smell were still fully functional.

The Great Hall was cloaked in silence. There were faint sounds of people padding past her, getting into position, and whispering for complete quiet. Irene blocked out those sounds, concentrating on getting her bearings.

The fragrant odor of burning wood in the stone fireplace came from directly behind her. Aromas of cloves and cinnamon drifted toward her from the dessert table on her right. Just orienting herself calmed her a little.

She wondered if Logan was present, then shook the notion from her thoughts. He wasn't here. He wouldn't play such a silly game. He had more important things on his mind. He was making sure his mother was okay.

Someone guided her away from the fireplace. She

73

knew it was Bridget because of the gentle scent of gardenias. "Are you ready to meet the first contestant?" Bridget said. When Irene nodded, Bridget placed Irene's hand on a man's shoulder. He was about Irene's height. She felt him lean forward and kiss her.

The sensation of his lips on hers was quick and abrupt. Like it might feel if she had kissed the back of her own hand. Irene shook her head, and pressed her lips together. Bridget guided her to the next guy. The second man seemed more formal. He gave her a peck on each check.

The next few men were a blur. One went in for a second kiss, but that was against the rules, and Bridget ordered him to leave and whisked Irene to the next man. The faint smells of spices filled the air as each kiss brought her closer to the dessert table. She knew the procedure now. Hand on the man's shoulder, lean in, touch lips, wait for a reaction, and then move on to the next candidate.

The whole experience gave her time to analyze her own dating merry-go-round ride. Of course, physical attraction was part of the equation, but did she rely on it too much?

She realized she'd ignored some of the early warning signs with her ex-fiancé. She'd believed his excuses for the unexpected trips and the late nights at the office because, if she was being honest, her ex was movie-star gorgeous and successful. Even the shock of finding him with another woman hadn't woken her the first time she'd caught him. After all, he'd vowed to change.

Their relationship had been such a sad cliché.

Her sister had finally penetrated the denial-fog she

had been in with the simple question: "What would Mother say?"

As Bridget guided Irene's hand onto the next candidate's shoulder, she sensed that she was back to where she'd started. The man was taller than the others, his muscles more defined. She rose on tiptoes and tilted her head back, knowing he'd have to bend down to reach her. She didn't have a strong enough hold on his shoulder and started to fall.

The man placed his hand on the small of her back to steady her. The protective gesture caught her off guard. She was the one who watched out for her co-workers and friends. Not the other way around.

He pressed his lips against hers, igniting a spark that took her by surprise.

The spark ignited into flame. She leaned in and deepened the kiss as his arms pulled her closer. Heat spiraled around her in ever-increasing speed. Enveloped in his embrace, she sensed the world dropping away. The only sound was her beating heart. An image of Logan flickered through her thoughts. But what if it wasn't him?

A roar of laughter, mixed with a round of clapping and cheers, penetrated the haze as Bridget pulled Irene gently from her mystery man.

Irene knew the chill of loss. She hugged her arms around her waist and waited to find out his identity.

"The heart knows," Bridget said as she untied Irene's blindfold.

Irene kept her eyes shut as she clung to the fantasy. She wanted the man to be Logan. There didn't seem to be any drama around him. The expression "What you see is what you get" came to mind. Was that real? Or part of the fantasy?

Bridget nudged her on the shoulder. "He's waiting."

Irene opened her eyes, rubbing them, more to delay the moment than any real need to focus. She wanted to see clearly. Doubts rushed in. Was that even possible when it came to the emotions of the heart?

She looked at the tips of her shoes first and then saw his leather boots.

Nondescript and like every other pair of boots she'd seen at this thirteenth century reenactment festival.

He wore a green tunic, which narrowed the field a bit. Her heart picked up speed.

Broad shoulders.

She felt out of breath, as though she were running through a snowstorm in a gale-force wind. Slow down, she cautioned.

Square jaw. Lips that curved in a familiar smile that shone in his eyes.

Her first reaction was excitement; the second was paralyzing terror.

"Logan." His name rushed out as the doubts swept over her again. How was it possible to feel so much for someone so soon?

Chapter Nineteen

Irene twisted away from Logan and fled from the Great Hall, racing up the stairs to the balcony. It was a setup. Logan was someone the matchmakers must have planned for her all along. But how could they know there'd be an attraction? Were the sisters that good? More importantly, why was she so resistant? And why had she run away?

After all, the fantasy would be over in the morning, and things would be back to normal. Pretense. Fantasy. Make believe. Wasn't that what life was about anyway? If you knew that the person you loved had flaws, you ignored them. If your friends or family brought those flaws to your attention, you either said the guy you were dating had changed or he was working on his issues—or you got new friends.

The illusion of perfection. That had been the way she'd dealt with her relationship with Chad.

Almost from the beginning she'd realized they hadn't been right for each other. And the more her friends and family highlighted his flaws, the more she dug in and defended him. She developed the philosophy that the best way to sustain a relationship was never to look too closely at the person you were with.

And then there was Logan. There had to be something wrong with him. No one was perfect.

When she reached the balcony, she peered over the

waist-high ledge and removed her headdress and hair clips, leaving only a ribbon to control her long hair. From her vantage point, she could see that the celebrations in the Great Hall were continuing in full swing. Caitlin had volunteered to participate in the kissing game, while Angus stood on the sidelines, arms folded across his chest, and frowned in disapproval. A twelve-foot fir tree had been brought in, and although it would be centuries before ornaments and candles were added, its appearance added Christmas joy. A fiddler played a lively tune, which had led to impromptu dancing. Grant had coaxed Julia into a circle of dancers.

Sean and Ann stood hand in hand, shoulders touching, as they swayed in time to the music. Even if you didn't know them, you could tell they cared deeply for each other. What would it be like to share that type of for-ever-after kind of love with another person?

Arms resting on the ledge, Irene's thoughts drifted with the laughter. She knew her mother had cared for her stepfather. They were comfortable with each other, her mother had once said. Was that enough? Was that what she should be looking for in a man? Maybe forego all the thrill and excitement of love and settle for comfortable? *Mother, what secrets are you hiding?*

"I was looking for you."

Startled, Irene let her veil slip from her grasp as she turned toward him. "Logan."

His gaze followed the path of her headdress as it floated down into the Great Hall. "I could get it for you."

Her lips still felt warm from the kiss they'd shared. What must he think of her running away? Feeling self-conscious, she laughed nervously. "I can retrieve it later."

He gave a curt nod. "You let your hair down."

She laughed again. "I suppose I did." Seconds ticked by. He stood as though rooted to the ground. He was tall, straight, and as solid as an oak. A man you could depend on. A man you could build a life with. "I wonder what he does for fun." She thought she'd said it to herself, but when his head jerked toward her with a smile, she realized she'd voiced her thoughts aloud.

His gaze warmed. "I play rugby. But my father says I need a hobby that doesn't include broken bones and bruised ribs. How about you?"

Irene bit back a smile. "No time. I work. Of late, I've been thinking I should rethink that philosophy. It's time I found a hobby, too." She brushed her fingers over the seams on the stone ledge. "Our kiss…"

He moved in closer and covered her hand with his. "I had the advantage. I've wanted to kiss you since I first saw you move to defend the waitress in the café from the bottom feeders who were harassing her. You were fearless."

The compliment was sincere. She could tell it in his gaze. People had said good things about her over the years: hard worker, efficient, organized. Never fearless. She liked the possibility that she'd tapped into a new strength. Was it this place? Stirling Castle was so far removed from her life in the States and who she was that it felt like she had the chance to become the person she'd always wanted to be.

Her pulse quickened until she could feel it vibrate through her. Out of breath, she lifted her head until their gazes locked. Instinctively she knew Logan wouldn't make the first move to kiss her. He stood waiting as though he could wait for an eternity.

In the background, music and laughter defined the boundaries of the room while the promise of love beat around her. She moved to meet him as he bent toward her, closing the distance.

Their lips parted and touched.

If the first kiss they'd shared was the spark of awakening, the second was an explosion. Her world spun in all directions at the same time as she wrapped her arms around his neck. He gathered her against him and deepened the kiss.

Chapter Twenty

This was Lady Roselyn's favorite time of the evening. The kitchens were quiet, and the guests were busy getting to know one another. On the far side, a wall was devoted to a walk-in hearth, where lamb stew bubbled happily in an iron pot. A baking oven stood nearby, and pies cooled beneath an open window.

The fragrance of cinnamon, nutmeg, and cloves drifted through the air as Lady Roselyn broke off a corner of pie crust and popped it into her mouth. The butter-rich flavor was therapeutic. Chocolate would have been better, but it wasn't available in thirteenth-century Europe. It would take a few hundred years for it to cross the Atlantic. First, Cortez had to discover it in the New World. He'd introduce it to the court. After his presentation, the one that began with Montezuma drinking it before he visited his harem and ended with the number of wives, concubines, and children Montezuma had, the court would declare chocolate a powerful aphrodisiac. The next step, quite predictably, was the decree that it was too dangerous for women to consume, which of course only made everyone want it more.

She sighed, wishing she had smuggled a dark chocolate bar with sea salt and caramel into her purse, but, as head matchmaker, she couldn't break the rules. She dusted off her hands and turned toward Bridget.

Her sister was attacking the dough as though it were the enemy.

"Something is wrong," Bridget said. "I can feel it."

Lady Roselyn reached for another piece of pie crust. "You worry too much."

"Isn't that what I should be saying to you?" Bridget rubbed more flour on the rolling pin and bent again over her task. "We've invited too many this time. The limit is five. We have seven."

"You're the one who kept adding sprinkles to everyone's hot cocoa."

Bridget wiped her forehead with the back of her hand, smudging flour over her face. "What was I supposed to do? You know the rules. I couldn't refuse anyone, once Fiona suggested sprinkles to them. Besides, how was I to know that everyone who asked for them would also agree to the Matchmaker Tour? That's never happened before."

Lady Roselyn pinched off more crust. "Well, it's happened now, and we're going to have to live with it. All we have to do is get through the staged attack on the castle and the wedding later this evening. Are Caitlin and Angus ready?"

Bridget lined another pie plate with the newly rolled-out crust and filled it with sliced apples. "Define ready. Caitlin is threatening to call it off. When she participated in our kissing game, she sent a clear signal. She said Angus lied to her about his relationship with Julia. We don't know if Caitlin was just trying to make Angus jealous or if this is the beginning of the end. Fiona is with her now, trying to repair the damage, but you know Fiona. If she has the slightest doubt of a couple's love or commitment, she'll persuade them to at least slow things down. She might even ask them to postpone the wedding. One more thing. Fiona and Liam aren't speaking. Again."

"Fabulous." Lady Roselyn heaved a sigh. "Their arranged betrothal has been a problem since it was first announced. First things first. If we survive, we're going to have to change how we select our couples, or at the least choose less volatile locations. There has to be a better way of selecting the groups, as well. Seven is too unwieldy. We can't keep track of them all: they keep wandering off, or falling in and out of love. Why can't everyone be more like Sean and Ann? Now, there's a couple who understands what it takes to sustain a relationship. We need our happily-ever-after ending. We need a wedding. What are we going to do if there isn't one?"

Bridget finished the lattice-work top on her pie, set it aside, and went over to the window to see if the pies there had cooled. "We could ask for an extension."

Lady Roselyn heaved a sigh. "The enchantment on this castle doesn't work that way."

Bridget put her hands on her hips. "That's odd. I could have sworn I made more pies. Three are missing."

Chapter Twenty-One

The library was darker and colder than Irene remembered, or maybe it was the anticipation of locating the portrait Logan described that made it feel more foreboding. Regardless, she loved that he'd found an excuse for them to steal away from the group. Irene blew on her hands to warm them as Logan added another log to the fire.

He brushed off his hands and eased away from the hearth. "Are you ready?"

She fought the impulse to shake her head. When he patiently waited for her response, as though he'd guessed her unease, she felt familiar warmth settle around her. Somehow he'd suspected her apprehension. It felt as though she'd known him much longer than a handful of hours. She wanted to ask him if he felt the same, or was it crazy to believe in the possibility of soulmates. She settled on a safer question.

"What do you think it will mean? That is, if the likeness is as similar as you say?"

Logan took both her hands in his and smiled. "I know you're trying to prepare yourself for any scenario. Very analytical. If I were to narrow down toward a potential occupation for you, I'd say you were a research scientist, lawyer, accountant, computer programmer, writer... Am I getting warm?"

She mirrored his smile, impressed at his guesses. "I

thought we weren't to tell each other our occupations."

He squeezed her hands. "I couldn't help myself. It's part of my curious nature. This portrait that looks so much like your mother also started me thinking. Maybe we have to live with the fact that we might never find an explanation for everything. Like why people are afraid of clowns or enjoy the thrill of swimming with sharks."

Irene reached up and kissed him lightly. "Just for the record, I love clowns but draw the line when it comes to swimming with sharks. You're quite the philosopher."

"Me and Snoopy." His grin grew serious. "It's okay to change your mind about finding the portrait. I mean, I'm sure I'm overthinking the resemblance."

"Except that the woman was also wearing earrings that resemble my pendant."

"A puzzle."

"Or the beginning of a nightmare."

Chapter Twenty-Two

The good news was that torches were set in wall sconces along the corridors. The bad news was that because all the corridors looked the same, Irene was concerned they were walking in circles.

Afraid of getting lost, she employed a trick she used when visiting a new city. Most people kept track of street signs. Irene had a different method. She studied the fashions in the display windows. This strategy was particularly effective when you visited a country where you weren't familiar with the language on the street signs. Usually no two displays in shop windows were exactly alike, and the same could be said of the portraits in the corridors.

While the facial features began to blur, the clothing of the men and women pictured was distinctive. As varied as the people in an international airport, the clothes ranged from unadorned muted colors to finery with elaborate headdresses that rivaled those worn by King Henry the Eighth or his daughter Elizabeth the First and her cousin Mary Queen of Scots. The frames surrounding each portrait were as diverse as the subjects themselves, from simple wood frames to ones carved and gilded with gold or silver.

When they rounded a corner, Logan quickened his pace. His expression lit up like a boy who'd learned he was going to meet his favorite rugby player. "Here we are." He lifted a torch from the wall sconce and brought it near the portrait of a woman. She wore a gown with long sleeves embroidered with sprigs of lavender and earrings shaped like snowflakes.

"What do you think?" Logan said.

The whisper of a chill brushed her skin. "Can you bring the torch in closer?"

When he did, it cast a beam of light over the portrait while plunging the surrounding area in shadows. The portrait was surrounded by a wide silver frame, etched with the same images embroidered in the woman's gown.

Irene moved in closer. The woman was in her mid-twenties, lovely, relaxed, happy. Irene reached out to almost touch the face, but she closed her fingers and pulled back at the last moment. "It's not possible," she whispered under her breath.

"The resemblance is just a coincidence, right?" Logan said. "Or maybe it's one of your great-great-great-great ancestors. Did I use the correct amount of greats?"

"I'm not sure…" Irene felt as though the floor had dropped out from under her. "The resemblance is spooky."

"Maybe the earrings are a family heirloom."

"Maybe," Irene repeated. She kept nodding, knowing she was trying to believe Logan's logic. But she wasn't sure. The resemblance was too similar. Irene touched the birthmark on the corner of her mouth, the one both her sister and her mother had. The same birthmark was visible on the woman in the picture.

She reached out for Logan. She needed an anchor. A safe place. Something solid. "I know this sounds crazy, but I think my mother was here."

****

After seeing what looked like her mother's portrait, Irene walked in a daze. Each corridor they traveled down looked like the last. Stone and mortar that looked newer than it should. Tapestries that were vibrant in color, not faded with age. Logan had asked her what she meant when she said she thought her mother had been to the castle. She'd deflected his question.

Irene's intention was to return to the Great Hall and confront the matchmakers. Her mother had never traveled to a foreign country, but even if she had, she'd never have kept it a secret from her family. Why would she? This was a simple case of someone looking like her mother. Irene would explain this all to the matchmakers. They would calm her down and tell her she had a wild imagination. They would also discount Julia's ridiculous theory of time travel. Of course, if Louise had been along, she'd have leapt at Julia's theory. When they were children, Julia was the one claiming she saw fairy wings on the neighbor's kittens. Irene was the practical one.

She paused, hands on hips. "Wait a second. I don't think we went this way before. We're lost. I don't get lost."

Logan rubbed the back of his neck. "I agree. None of this looks familiar."

Irene nodded absently, reaching out to run her hand over the stone wall to her right. It was different from the others she'd seen along the way. In the center of each stone were raised images of plants, flowers, or small forest creatures. "I've seen a picture of this before." She reached for the diary. "My mother made a drawing of this wall." Irene flipped through it until she found the page.

Logan looked over her shoulder. "The caption says this is a hidden entrance to a series of passageways that crisscross behind the walls of the castle. Sounds like a great way to surprise an enemy who has infiltrated the castle, and then the opportunity for the inhabitants to escape."

Irene turned to the next page. A series of diagrams mapped the passageways and where they led. The labyrinth of tunnels seemed to connect to every chamber in the castle. "That may have been its original intent, but it also became a common way for lovers to sneak into each other's rooms undetected. Kings visited their mistress and queens the noblemen who caught their fancy, as they called it."

"Caught their fancy," Logan repeated with a grin. Old-fashioned sayings are the best, and they fit you somehow. Have I caught your fancy?"

She felt the heat of a blush warm her checks. How could she answer him without exposing her heart again?

Logan came around to face Irene, tucking a strand of hair behind her ear. His fingers brushed the curve of her face. "I put you on the spot. Sorry. I couldn't help it. It must be this place." He paused. "And you. I sense you're a romantic at heart. You find the romance in everything. Everyone focuses on the monster Grendel in *Beowulf*, but you wonder about the hero, wonder about Beowulf and who he loved. I think the hidden walls in this castle are a battle strategy. You think of someone being able to find true love. Strangest thing. When I'm around you, I have the impulse to try on a suit of armor and defend you with my life."

Warmed by his gaze, Irene rested her hand on his arm, feeling his muscles react to her touch. "I've never thought of myself in that way before. You bring out the romance in me, too."

His lips parted, and his hand pressed against the small of her back and drew her to him, closing his eyes. The pressure of his mouth on hers brought back the excitement of their first kiss. Each time with him felt like the first time. Would it always feel this way? She shut her eyes, chasing away such thoughts. For once she wanted to live in the moment. Always before, she had tried to predict the future. On more than one occasion she'd had the location of the honeymoon and the names of her children picked out before the end of a first date. Not this time. This time she wanted it to be different.

She leaned in, and the kiss deepened, erasing all thoughts except of the man who held her in his arms.

Moments later, he drew back, kissed her eyelids and then the tip of her nose, his breath a warm caress. His eyes reflected the fire in the torches on the wall. She knew the silent question he asked. Another place, another time, she might have said yes. But the magic of Stirling Castle and the stories her mother had written about her time here wrapped around her like a warm cloak. Irene's life had always been on the fast track. For once she wanted to embrace the idea of going slow, experiencing what it meant to be courted by someone who made her heart warm each time she thought or said his name. She wanted chivalry. She wanted her knight in shining armor.

That he'd waited for her answer made her believe the magic of the castle had spoken to him, as well. "I'm in the mood for an adventure. Would you like to explore the hidden passageways my mother mentioned?"

The slow rise of the corner of his mouth into a grin said it all as he reached for her hand. She loved that he always did that. She loved that the gesture felt so natural. Most of all, she loved that his expression said he could wait.

He scratched the back of his neck. "Any ideas how we get this wall to open?"

Irene stepped in front of him, examining the wall and her mother's drawings. It looked like a solid wall of stone. There weren't any visible outlines of a door. "We could say, 'Open sesame.' "

He cocked his head. "Pretty sure that's a different story. I'm thinking there's probably some sort of a mechanism that releases the door's latch if you press in the right place. All we have to do is find it. Any clues in your mother's diary?"

Irene looked closer. "There's a drawing of a Scottish thistle."

Logan eyed the drawing. "I've seen those everywhere around here. They reminded me of the same bristle-like haircut my eight-grade gym teacher had. Wait a minute." Logan traced his hand over the raised images on the stones until he found what he was looking for. He pressed down in the center of the stone and heard a click.

The solid wall moved inward, letting out a draft of cold, stale air.

Chapter Twenty-Three

Irene kept her hand on Logan's shoulder as they descended the stairs in single file. He held a torch that helped a little. She didn't know which was worse, walking in complete darkness down an uneven staircase or watching shadows caused by the torchlight flicker over the walls.

Shadows crawled overhead, creating a dark canopy of gloom. Metal crashing onto stone echoed through the narrow passageway, sending the shadows into hiding.

Logan paused.

"You heard it too."

"This passageway doesn't feel like it leads to the chambers in the castle. We keep going down." He held the torch higher.

"Probably just critters, running from the light," she offered, her teeth chattering with the cold.

"You mean rats."

"No, I most definitely mean critters. Critters are cute, like rabbits, or the mice in the story of Cinderella. Rats and spiders…" She shuddered, knowing she was talking too fast. "Rats and spiders are just plain creepy."

Logan's soft laughter echoed over the walls. "Critters it is, then. Do you want to turn back and…" His last words were drowned out by the muffled shouts of men's voices.

"Stay close," Logan said as he advanced. His voice had deepened, and his lips compressed into a thin line.

"Who do you think they are?"

"Could be the castle staff."

She heard the doubt in his voice as they reached the last step. It opened into a circular stone room with high ceilings. A neglected fire pit lay in the center, its dying embers giving off enough light to illuminate a bank of cells on the right.

Logan raised his torch. "What's Sam doing here?"

At the far end, Sam was unlocking one of the cells. Three men poured out and glanced in Irene and Logan's direction. Irene recognized the three men at once. They were the same men who had harassed Bridget in the Matchmaker Café.

Logan pulled Irene behind him as Sam advanced toward them. The three men spread out to their left and right.

"Hey, guys," Sam said. "What're you doing down here?"

"Lost." Logan's voice was devoid of emotion. "Care to point the way out of here?"

"The only way out is the way you came in," Sam said. "Clever builders, these Scots. One entrance in or out assured their prisoners stayed put. But I can't allow you to leave. We've had a little misunderstanding with the sisters we have to sort out, and you'd spoil the surprise. Can't risk you telling the sisters what you've seen." Sam jangled a set of keys. "I apologize in advance. I don't think you'll like your new accommodations."

Logan's voice was deadly calm. "Let me get this straight. Your plan is to lock us in a cell?" His manner reminded Irene of how he'd been in the café earlier today.

"Nothing personal. Just until we get what we want." Sam motioned to the three men he'd released. They moved in toward Sam.

Logan kept his focus on Sam. "The men you released are the ones I dealt with in the café. Poor choice in friends. But I'm curious—do you think there are rats and spiders in the cell?"

Sam looked confused. "I think so…"

Logan shrugged. "Well, that's going to be a problem. Being locked up doesn't work for me. Not a fan of cramped spaces, and Irene doesn't like rats or spiders." Logan glanced over his shoulder toward Irene. "You don't, do you?"

She shook her head slowly. Irene had no idea where this was going except Logan's expression looked like it was forged from iron. He handed her the torch. Then he winked and mouthed, "Get ready to run."

He turned back to Sam. "Sorry, by the way."

"For what?"

"For this." Logan rolled his fists, hit Sam in the jaw with one and in the stomach with the other. The three men rushed forward, but Irene swung the torch back and forth, keeping them at bay. Logan grabbed the moaning Sam and shoved him into the three men. They all toppled over into a heap like bowling pins as Logan grabbed Irene's hand and ran.

Chapter Twenty-Four

The staircase didn't look familiar and neither had the corridors they'd just left. Somewhere along the way, in escaping Sam and his comrades, they'd made a wrong turn, and instead of going back up, they were going down again. As though she and Logan ran from bad guys on a daily basis, she took the lead, and he made sure they weren't being followed.

When the staircase made a sharp turn, and widened, there was a cluster of narrow windows. She didn't remember seeing those on their way to the library or in the secret passage to the dungeons. So much for her foolproof way of not getting lost.

The ceiling over the staircase lowered abruptly. She ducked her head and shouted over her shoulder. "Logan, watch your…

A split second later she heard a loud thunk, followed by a muffled curse as a thin mist of powdery rocks and mortar rained down on them.

"Too late," Logan shouted back, rubbing his head.

Irene brushed the fragments of rock from his hair. "Are you okay?"

"Are you?"

She knew they weren't talking about the bump on his head. "I think I'm still trying to process what happened. It seems odd that the men from the café were locked up. I thought they were just asked to leave. I'm unfamiliar with the laws in Scotland, but locking them up seems extreme under the circumstances, and what was Sam doing releasing them, if the sisters did have them put there in the first place?"

"Nothing good."

"Agreed. Thank you for saving me, by the way."

He grinned. "All part of a knight's duty to his lady. But the way I see it, we were a team. You were pretty fierce."

"Not sure I know where that came from."

"I do." He paused, then added, "We should keep going."

Warmed by his compliments, she continued down the stairs. "Remember to keep your head low."

"I guess when this castle was built, people weren't very tall."

"For the most part you're right," Irene said, remembering an entry in her mother's diary. "But William Wallace was over six feet tall, and I think Mary Queen of Scots was five feet eleven. The real reason for the low ceilings and uneven steps was to slow the enemy down. The placement of the rope hand railing was also strategic. Most people are right-handed, so the hand railing was placed on the right side going up, so anyone attacking and running up the stairs would have to shift their weapons to their left hand, giving the castle guards advancing from above an advantage."

He chuckled. "Having you along is like having my own personal tour guide."

"Sorry."

"Don't be. You're passionate about history. I can hear it in your voice. I'll bet you're a great teacher."

For some reason she didn't want to correct him. As

a child, she would line up her dolls and teach them about the great queens and women warriors of ancient and modern times. She'd make crowns and swords out of cardboard and wrap them in tinfoil. When she was older, she'd abandoned her dream of teaching, and to this day she wasn't sure why. Funny, she hadn't thought about that part of her life in a long time.

"Both my grandmother and mother were teachers," she said, knowing she really hadn't answered his question—or her own, for that matter.

"Do you know why this place was so important to your mother?" He paused. "Or more to the point, to you?"

Irene continued down the stairs, not sure how to answer his question. Before she left Seattle, her goal had seemed easy: find out why Stirling Castle figured so prominently in her mother's diary. A major part of her believed that her mother had made it all up. Louise hadn't liked that theory, probably the reason she'd done everything she could to get Irene here, short of pushing Irene onto the plane. Now that she was here, more questions kept bubbling to the surface, like why did her mother and the woman in the portrait look so much alike? Were the earrings connected? And then there was the birthmark. Did they really have a lookalike relative? Too many coincidences. Some people didn't believe in coincidences. Her mother had been one of them. The biggest question still remained. Who was Connor?

She reached out to the wall for balance as the staircase took another sharp turn. "My sister and I thought we knew everything there was to know about our mother. After her death, her diary was included in the paperwork we received along with her will. For some reason, she couldn't share her secrets with us while she was living, and my sister and I wanted to know the reason why. Our stepfather thinks we have unresolved mother issues. The classic 'she didn't spend enough time reading bedtime stories' or 'she expected us to be perfect.' And the big one, 'she died so we felt abandoned.' Except the only one of those scenarios that came close was the last one. My sister and I miss her every day."

"This is going to sound odd, but in a way I know exactly how you feel. Yes, my mother is still alive, but because of Alzheimer's, there are times when I feel she's already left me and my dad. I want to try and reason with her not to leave. To stay. To see me. If I thought she'd also kept secrets, I'd be curious, if only to get closure to unanswered questions. Why do you think your mother left you the diary in the first place?"

Irene paused to look over her shoulder toward him. Light and shadow reflected off his features. The smoke and age-stained walls faded into the background until the only clear image was of Logan.

She turned to face him in the tight confines of the staircase. He was so close his breath warmed the chilled air. She'd not expected to feel so much in such a short span of time. Her journey here was about closure. Instead it had opened up a flood of emotions. "I wish I knew the answer. But other than my sister, you're the only person who's asked me that question. My sister and I knew our mother only in her role as mom. She never lived long enough for us to have the chance to become friends. When she knew she was dying, I think she felt the same sense of loss." Irene's words trailed off.

Logan reached out for her hand. She nodded and let out a breath. "I'm okay. I'm starting to think my mother's diary was a way for her to bridge that gap. I just wonder why she felt she had to keep her time here a secret."

Her words caught in the air and lingered. Irene continued the rest of the way down the stairs in silence broken only by the sound of her footfalls and the lingering question in her thoughts. What if the real reason her mother had kept the truth a secret was that she was afraid of what her daughters might discover?

With each step the passageway narrowed and the closer it came to the ground floor. When Irene neared the last step, the air chilled and her breath frosted the air. The staircase ended at a thick door rounded at the top and studded with iron rivets. A crossbar lay horizontally across the door and was secured in place by metal hooks.

"We keep getting lost," Irene announced.

"We could retrace our steps?"

"Except we're lost."

Logan grinned and blew on his hands. "Well, there is that. I'm actually enjoying this adventure. The best things happen when you're not looking."

Her first impulse was to look for sarcasm in his expression. Instead, she found something unexpected. Smoldering like a banked fire was desire. Had a man ever looked at her in that way before? She shook her head, answering her own question. Her skin flushed. "You are weird." Irene groaned at her response. She sounded like a teenager talking to her first crush.

He winked. "Not the worst thing I've been called."

"I'm not going to ask. But unlike you, I don't like

feeling this way. I mean…feeling lost."

"You mean feeling out of control?" he joked.

She didn't really know if that was what she'd meant. She did know that she loved their easy banter. She anchored her hands on her hips in mock protest. "There's nothing wrong with wanting to be in control."

He raised his hands in surrender. "Don't misunderstand. I understand completely what you're going through. My dad thinks I invented the label 'control freak.' One of the issues on my list of things to fix."

Irene fought back a smile. "Sounds like you have a long list."

"You have no idea. So what's the plan?"

Pausing to take in how well he'd come to know her in such a short time, she said, "You're supposing that I have a plan."

"Don't you?"

"Of course. Just testing." Irene nodded toward the door. "I suggest we open the door and go around to the front of the castle and enter through the café and changing rooms. From there it seemed like a straight shot to the Great Hall." Irene tried the door handle beneath the crossbar, but it was locked. "How good are you at picking locks?"

Logan removed the crossbar and placed the palm of his hand against the wood, giving it a testing push. "I could break it down?"

"Really? These doors are solid oak. At least six to eight inches thick."

He arched an eyebrow and grinned. "Your point?"

She knew he was joking. Well, that wasn't exactly true. So far, this was a very unorthodox tour experience, to say the least.

Logan ran his hand over the wood panels. "All kidding aside, you're right about the door. I thought it would be weaker because it was at least three or four hundred years old, but the panels look almost brand new and the iron hinges newly forged."

"The brochure said most of the castle was restored."

"Have you wondered why there always seems to be a logical explanation?" he said absently. Logan turned the handle. It wouldn't budge. "If the builders replicated the locks exactly as they were from the thirteenth century, picking it shouldn't be that difficult." Logan reached under his belt and produced a Swiss army knife he'd attached by a cord. He flipped open the nail file.

"The sisters would be upset if they knew you brought something from modern times."

He cast her a sly grin. "You needed your mother's diary, and I never go anywhere without my knife." Logan knelt down, inserted the nail file in the lock, and turned it. There was a clicking sound. He pulled back and put his knife away. "Moment of truth, as they say." He turned the handle and pulled the door open slowly.

Wisps of snow drifted through the opening on a current of cold air.

Surrounded by the swirling snow, Logan stood as still as the statues of the knights that guarded the Great Hall. His muscles tensed. "Something's not right."

Chapter Twenty-Five

A blast of ice-cold air forced the door open wider. It banged against the wall. Drifts of snow continued to rush in as Irene and Logan fought to close the door. The wind pushed back. Logan let out a roar of his own and slammed his shoulder against the door, sealing the entrance. Irene braced to hold the door shut while he pushed the crossbar down on the metal hooks. When it was secured, Irene leaned with her back against the wall, catching her breath.

A winter storm was not unusual in late December. Her weather app, however, had predicted a light dusting of snow, not a full-blown blizzard.

Irene rubbed her arms to get warm. "I wonder if the matchmakers will let us spend the night. My taxi driver promised he'd be here when the tour ended, but I can't imagine he'd be able to make it out in this weather."

Logan's eyebrows knitted together, and he nodded. His gaze was still locked on the closed door.

When he didn't respond she began to worry. It wasn't like him to be so quiet. "What did you mean when you said that something wasn't right?"

Logan brushed the back of his hand across his forehead and stepped away from the door. "I must be seeing things. I think it's this place. That whole incident in the dungeon with Sam and the men he freed...and the fact that the castle and all its furnishings and tapestries are new rather than hundreds of years old. This feels too real. It's messing with my mind." He gave a nervous laugh. "Does that make sense?"

Irene knew that feeling all too well. They hadn't talked very much about the men who'd tried to lock them in the dungeon. For her part, she hadn't wanted to believe she and Logan had been in any real danger. She wanted to believe that it was all part of the tour experience the matchmakers talked about. But Logan had taken it seriously…

"You think Sam really meant to lock us in the dungeon?"

"And throw away the key," Logan said.

"I did some reading about this place and the elaborate reconstruction over the centuries. Yet there's no sign of it anywhere. Does that seem strange to you?"

"As strange as what I *didn't* see outside just now. All the directional and informational signs that were visible when we came here earlier are missing."

"Maybe they're covered in snow or blew over."

He cocked an eyebrow. "But did I mention there were at least twenty horses and men with bows and arrows aimed at the castle?"

She looked at him, trying to process what he was saying. "Perhaps they're actors, planning a mock attack. The sisters talked about wanting to give our tour an experience we wouldn't forget. Maybe it's all part of the celebrations for Christmas Eve."

Logan shook his head slowly. "Those men didn't look like they were in a holiday mood. They looked like they were planning to storm the castle."

"You're overreacting. Maybe we both are."

He rubbed the shoulder he'd used to slam the door

closed. "First, you don't look like the type, and second, do I look like someone who overreacts?"

"Well, no," Irene said. "You look like someone who analyzes the pros and cons of any given situation."

He nodded. "My mother used to say it was both a flaw and a blessing. If I'm unsure about something, I'll examine every angle before I rush in. On the other hand, if I'm convinced down to my toes that something is right, I jump in with both feet. And right now I'm in the examining-all-angles stage. What I do suspect is that somehow Sam and those men he freed are involved, and it's not good. It's time we took a closer look."

****

Irene and Logan had retraced their steps up the winding staircase to the landing where they had a clear view of the courtyard. Cold air seeped through the narrow opening before her, chilling Irene's fingers. A storm raged, and the torchlight on the castle walls cast only a miser's glow over the courtyard. Shadows moved and twisted in the strengthening wind, fueling her imagination. They looked like soldiers. Irene stamped down her overactive thoughts.

"I think what you saw was a trick of shadows," Irene said hopefully. "No one would be out in this weather."

"Only a person up to no good," Logan added as he stood beside her.

Pinpricks of light moved amongst the shadows. She peered closer as her eyes adjusted to the darkness. A flash of steel burned through the snowdrifts. The shadows increased in numbers as they moved toward the castle. The muffled sounds of marching moved with them. The shadows took shape. Men carrying torches were grouped together a short distance away. The men were armed with medieval weapons and shields. She might not understand what they were saying, but as they shook their fists at the castle, there was no denying their intentions. They were preparing for an attack.

The faint clip-clop gait of hooves over cobblestones echoed over the courtyard, and the outline of a horse-drawn wagon came into view. A man with a wide-brimmed hat that looked like it had been soaked in mud snapped the reins on the rump of the sway-backed animal and shouted something unintelligible.

Logan moved in closer beside her. "Can you hear what he's saying?"

Irene shrugged. "Not a clue. His Scottish accent is too thick."

A mangy dog sped out from behind the castle to nip at the horse's hooves. The man with the hat reined in his horse and shouted at the dog to get out of the way. He flipped aside the tarp, exposing an assortment of shields, swords, long bows, and lances. Three men came from behind the wagon. They patted each other on the back as they each reached in and selected a weapon.

Irene sucked in her breath.

"What is it?" Logan said.

"I can't see Sam, but the other three are the men he freed from the dungeon."

"Get back from the window!" Bridget shouted. She stood poised on the steps, out of breath. Her face was flushed and her eyes wild with fear. Instead of waiting for Irene and Logan to respond, she pulled them away from the window. Her hand trembled as she readjusted her veil. "I'm glad I found you." Her voice was thin and threaded with anxiety. "You'll miss the Christmas carols. Come along, now."

Irene knew a deflective tactic when she heard one. She'd had that strategy used on her more than once. Bridget was hiding something. She exchanged a glance with Logan. His expression seemed to mirror her own confusion. Something was going on, and it was clear that, whatever it was, Bridget was concerned.

Irene stood her ground. "Did you know there are men with bows and arrows aimed at the castle? I'm sure I recognized the men Logan confronted in the café earlier. The same men who were locked in a dungeon cell."

Bridget turned as white as the snowstorm outside the walls. Her mouth compressed in a thin line. "They escaped? It's worse than I thought. I told my sisters something like this might happen. You can't break the rules. That's the first rule."

Chapter Twenty-Six

Irene failed to coax answers from Bridget. Each question was met with either silence or a change in topic. The one good thing was that Bridget seemed to know exactly where she was going.

A shudder shook the staircase, and Irene braced her hands against the wall. Shards of stone and mortar rained over Irene's head in the cramped space. Somehow Irene managed to keep her balance as she glanced toward Logan. He was a few steps below her and was looking out one of the narrow windows.

"I didn't know they had earthquakes in Scotland."

Bridget shouldered past Irene and pulled Logan from the window. "We should keep going."

As though the matter were settled, Bridget sidestepped past Irene to resume the lead.

Logan reached for Irene to hold her back. "Did your mother mention earthquakes in her diary?"

"Not a word."

Bridget turned around. "Come along, now."

Another vibration let loose another stone shower. A trail of spider-web cracks spread along one of the windows.

"Follow me," Bridget shouted.

When they reached a wide area in the staircase, Bridget motioned for them to stop.

"Why are we stopping?"

107

"Shortcut." Bridget pressed on a raised wooden oval in the center of the door. It had the image of a Scottish thistle painted over the surface. The door clicked open onto a passageway.

"In the case of earthquakes," Irene said, "what's the protocol? Are you supposed to huddle under the strongest place in a dwelling, or is that for hurricanes and tornados? I'm from Seattle, and we don't have either of those. We have earthquakes, but so far the damage has been minimal. The worst one I've ever experienced was a four-point-five magnitude when I was visiting my sister. Pavement moved like ocean waves, which was a little freaky, but the buildings didn't topple over."

Irene knew she was rattling on and on. She also knew it was a defense mechanism her sister often used when she was nervous. It seemed to calm Louise, so maybe it would work for her.

Logan nodded toward Bridget. "That wasn't an earthquake, was it?"

Bridget opened her mouth to say something but then seemed to change her mind. "We should keep going."

"You keep saying that. So are you going to tell us what is happening, or do we get to guess? I was on a construction site recently where they used a wrecking ball to smash down the walls. That's what this feels like. Any chance they're tearing down the castle with us in it?"

"My sister, Lady Roselyn, will know what to do."

Chapter Twenty-Seven

Irene and Logan followed Bridget toward the matchmaker quarters near the Great Hall. Bridget had been quiet during the rest of the time it took to get there. Irene had tried to engage her in conversation, but she'd simply shaken her head and repeated that her sister had to be the one to answer any questions. Bridget kept muttering under her breath and pausing to look out the windows they passed along the way. Irene wasn't a party planner, but she'd attended enough weddings, baby showers, and going-away celebrations to suspect that this event had taken a sharp detour. As crazy as it had sounded at the time, Logan's wrecking ball theory sounded more plausible than an earthquake.

And Bridget, instead of denying the theory, had refused to respond.

When they neared their destination, Logan held back. He glanced in the direction of a bank of narrow windows that overlooked a wide expanse of meadowland and a copse of trees. "There are more lights than there were a few hours ago," he said, more to himself than to Irene.

"It's nighttime and Christmas Eve," Irene said with hope, thinking about the armed men she'd seen in the courtyard. "People turn on their lights when it gets darker."

Despite her explanation, she moved to where he

was standing. She'd learned from entries in her mother's diary that the narrow windows were referred to as arrow slits. Archers could attack the enemy below but still have a degree of protection from the surrounding walls. But how much protection would there be if the castle was under attack? She shook her head against the question. She was being paranoid and irrational. Despite Julia's claims to the contrary, this was the twenty-first century, not the thirteenth.

Logan held out his arm, preventing her from getting any closer. Keeping his gaze locked on the windows, he shouted, "Those aren't lights. They're flaming arrows, and they're headed straight toward us. Everyone get down!" He pulled Irene behind him as arrows arched toward the castle.

They were under attack. Most of the arrows struck the outside walls and bounced off.

However, more and more managed to sail through the windows, as though the archer's aim improved with each volley. One lodged in a man's leg, and one in the hem of a woman's skirt. People rushed to help them. Logan covered Irene with his body as flaming arrows shot past them.

Everything happened at once. Screams tore through the air. Shouts to close the shutters and a call to arms vibrated around her. More flaming arrows made it through and set a tapestry on fire. Irene jumped to her feet and helped Julia with the tapestry while Logan helped with the shutters. Other women rushed to help, and Irene recognized them as some of those who had served their dinner earlier.

Together they tore the tapestry from the wall and stomped out the flames before they spread. Fiona appeared out of nowhere with a drawn sword, accompanied by a tall man dressed in chainmail and armed with not only a sword but also a shield. Irene almost didn't recognize her, she seemed so different from the young woman in the ponytail who'd sold her a ticket for this tour.

The castle shook. The vibration was stronger than the ones they'd experienced on the stairwell. Another volley of arrows shot through the windows still unshuttered, and one grazed Logan's shoulder. His shirt caught on fire. Irene ripped one of the green-and-red banners from the wall, rushed to his side, and smothered the flames.

"Stand back," Bridget yelled as she raced over and threw a bucket of water over Logan. She bent down to examine the wound. "Minor burn. Nothing serious. The arrow grazed the skin, and the fire cauterized the wound." She patted him on the arm. "You'll be fine."

Irene ground her teeth together as she tore his shirt away from the wound. Bridget was right, the bleeding had stopped, but none of this should be happening. She was surrounded by a confusing mix of sights and sounds, each image more vivid than the last. The initial shock in those around her had worn off and had been replaced by a response to the call to arms as though the attack were as normal as rush hour traffic.

Shouts rose outside from the men attacking the castle.

"Surround the castle!"

"Those inside, prepare to die!"

Logan rolled to a sitting position, grimaced, and pushed to his feet, pulling Irene along with him. "I've attended my share of reenactment festivals in my time, and this is not that."

Bridget tossed Irene a clean shirt for Logan, spun around, and ran toward Fiona and the tall man, who someone had said was Liam. Lady Roselyn had arrived, as well, and looked as though she was going to burst into tears or faint or both. She kept pointing toward the side of the castle under attack. Fiona had sheathed her sword and rested one hand on the hilt of her blade. She was the picture of a warrior woman. The tall man at her side motioned to Angus and about a dozen men to follow him outside.

"You'll be fine," Logan said under his breath, repeating Bridget's words. He rolled his shoulder and grimaced again. "I've had a lot of injuries playing rugby. I can honestly say that a flaming arrow is a first. My guess is that the sisters were as surprised as we were."

"I agree." Irene's thoughts raced as fast as her beating heart as she helped him tear away what remained of the charred shirt. The attack felt too real. Was Julia right? Had they traveled back to the thirteenth century? She helped Logan put on the shirt Bridget had provided. "You keep saving me."

His grin was boyish as he kissed the tip of her nose. "It's an excuse to hold you in my arms." He retrieved the arrow from the ground and examined the feathers and shaft. A muscle flexed along his jaw. "Handmade. Not machine. They sure take their reenactments seriously around here."

Chapter Twenty-Eight

Then, as though someone had flipped a switch, the attack ended as quickly as it had begun. The aftermath was all that remained. Chairs and tables had been overturned in people's haste to escape the flaming arrows. Food littered the floors, and now that the chaos had ended, the wolfhounds were busy taking advantage of their good fortune. But the air was still charged like the moments after a lightning strike, as though everyone were counting down the seconds until they heard the roar of thunder.

Irene helped Julia, Caitlin, and Ann search out and care for the wounded, while Logan, his father, and Grant made sure all the doors and windows were secure.

Julia's words about traveling back to the thirteenth century rushed back again, this time with such force that Irene felt as though the wind had been knocked out of her. Was that even possible? It wasn't as though she hadn't heard of the concept. The theory was as common in pop culture as whipped cream was on hot chocolate. The modern day genius, Dr. Stephen Hawkins, who'd made black holes his life's work, once theorized that the laws of physics supported the possibility, no matter how unlikely.

A trumpet's blare brought the Great Hall to silence. Breathing deeply, Irene turned toward the sound.

113

Lady Roselyn, flanked by Bridget and Fiona, climbed the three steps to the raised platform. The Great Hall settled into an unnatural quiet. The eldest sister wore a pasted-on smile. "Wasn't that exciting?" Lady Roselyn announced. Her normal quiet, calm voice shook noticeably. "That is a taste of what those in the thirteenth century might have experienced on a day-to-day basis. Your enemy never takes a break, even during the Christmas season." She forced a laugh. "We should give our actors a round of applause." She waited for the crowd to comply with her suggestion. Only a few clapped, the effect half-hearted. "They put on a grand show," she continued raising her voice. "Have no fear; there won't be a repeat performance. One per tour, that's our motto. Good news. We are right on schedule. Preparations are already underway for our big feast at midnight."

Lady Roselyn, despite her positive spin, still looked shaken as she descended from the dais. Bridget followed closely, while Fiona stayed behind to talk with Caitlin. There was an awkward silence, and then activity resumed as people returned to the task of straightening up the Great Hall. Their haunted expressions spoke volumes.

Logan nodded to his father before heading toward Irene. He looked as worried as she felt. "Did you believe her?"

"Not a word. I think it's time we learned the truth."

Chapter Twenty-Nine

Irene motioned for Logan to follow her, and together they ran after the sisters. Instinct told her that of the three, Fiona, although a romantic at heart, held the tightest grip on her secrets and was the least likely to share what was going on. Lady Roselyn was a peacemaker and a strict observer of rules and schedules, and Bridget's first impulse was to try and help, even if it meant putting herself at risk. If Irene was to learn what was really going on, Bridget was her best bet.

She reached Bridget before she ducked into a chamber behind the Great Hall. "We'd like answers."

Bridget didn't look surprised; she looked tired, and there were dark smudges under her eyes. "My sister explained everything."

"I found my mother's portrait."

Bridget pulled on a loose thread on her sleeve. "I thought we… Can we talk about this later?"

A blanket of silence descended, but Irene stood firm. She'd come here for answers. "Who's Connor?"

A muscle by Bridget's eye twitched as she let out a breath. "Come with me."

Bridget ushered Irene and Logan into the massive chamber. A fire in the hearth sputtered and spit as it tried to blaze. Cubbyholes stuffed with scrolls of parchment lined the walls, reminding Irene of the library. But this wasn't a cozy library in the heart of a mansion or castle. Despite the style of furnishing, the room reminded Irene of the corporate offices and boardrooms of a Fortune Five Hundred company.

Below a candlelit chandelier, Lady Roselyn sat writing with a quill pen, looking like a queen doling out judgments. Her expression was pinched, as though she blamed herself for the attack.

Logan took Irene's hand. His presence made her feel less alone but did nothing to soothe her jangled nerves. Bridget's reaction to Irene finding her mother's portrait and the mention of Connor's name hadn't helped. It was as though she'd walked into a play in progress without knowing the plot, setting, or characters. If somehow Julia was correct and they'd traveled back in time, that possibility opened up more questions and concerns. Had her mother time traveled, as well? Her mother had been fascinated with Scotland in the thirteenth century. If what Julia said was true, that would explain a lot. But where did Connor fit in?

Bridget settled Irene and Logan on chairs, then approached Lady Roselyn. "What are we going to do?"

Lady Roselyn snatched off her glasses and pointed them toward Irene and Logan. "The real question is why did you bring them here?"

"Irene found her mother's portrait."

The eyeglasses Lady Roselyn held in her hand quivered. She lowered her voice. "I thought we took it down."

"I thought so too."

Lady Roselyn closed her eyes, rubbing the ridge of her nose. She breathed in and out, then lifted her chin and turned toward Irene. "From your reaction, it's obvious that you didn't know your mother also took one of our tours. We usually do a better job keeping track of our guests and protecting their secrets. I apologize. We should have taken down her portrait before you arrived." Lady Roselyn's voice sounded unnaturally calm, as though trying to coax someone off a ledge. Irene had the feeling the tone was not so much for Irene's benefit but that of Lady Roselyn and her sister.

"Your portrait will be ready before you leave," Lady Roselyn said. "Did you notice our painter when you arrived? Although he prefers to paint puppies and kittens—he says they're more appreciative—we also commission him to paint portraits of all our guests."

Lady Roselyn seemed to think that answered Irene's question and turned to whisper to Bridget, but her voice carried as Irene allowed what the matchmaker had said to sink in. Lady Roselyn had confirmed that Irene's mother had been here, despite her stepfather's claim that she had never traveled to Europe.

"Where is Fiona?" Lady Roselyn said in a hushed tone, intruding into Irene's thoughts. "We need everyone here."

Bridget rolled her shoulders, rubbing her neck. "I'm not sure. All I know is that the wedding between Caitlin and Angus has been called off…indefinitely. I told you that if Fiona didn't think the couple was ready…"

Lady Roselyn stood, slammed her palms on the table, and leaned forward. "And you're just telling me this now? You are aware that if we don't have a wedding, no one can leave."

"We were under attack," Bridget said evenly. "A bride who'd changed her mind seemed the least of our worries."

Lady Roselyn tightened her grip on her glasses. She seemed to notice Irene and Logan again and cleared her throat. "You should not have to listen to the details of running a business. Smooth as glass one day and rocky seas the next. Bridget, will you please see our guests to the kitchens and offer them sweet cakes and tea? We shouldn't bother them with our minor setbacks."

Bridget crossed her arms over her chest. "We can drop the charade. They already know things are not as they seem. Last time I checked, most tours do not include their guests being wounded with flaming arrows. But aside from the fact Irene knows her mother was here, I found Irene and Logan by the gatehouse door. They saw the men responsible for the attack, the same men we locked in the dungeon but who managed to escape. How did that happen? Did someone help them?"

"Sam helped them," Logan interrupted.

Both Bridget and Lady Roselyn snapped their attention toward him.

"He wanted to lock us in one of the dungeon cells, but we declined. I'm not a fan of cramped places, and Irene doesn't like spiders. You people really take your reenactments seriously around here. The attack on the castle looked real."

"It was real," Bridget said.

Lady Roselyn gripped her glasses so tightly they snapped. "I'll wager the villagers in Brigadoon never had this problem. There was always a wedding. No drama. No attacks. No…"

"A man was killed trying to escape Brigadoon.

That was pretty dramatic, sister dear," Bridget said.

Logan leaned in toward Irene and whispered. "What am I missing?"

Irene let out a shuddering breath. Julia had tried to tell her that their tour group had traveled to the thirteenth century. It had seemed crazy then. Now, not so much. And how was Brigadoon involved? That was in a made-up story where time stood still. A shiver chased over her skin.

When Logan repeated his question, she whispered. "Have you ever heard about an enchanted place called Brigadoon?"

Before he could answer, Lady Roselyn raised her voice and addressed Bridget.

"This is all your sister and Liam's fault. I told them we needed to access a different door through time. We've been returning to this same century for too long. We have more doors, more options, and we should start using them. We should also make a rule that under no circumstances should we allow our guests to use the same tour over and over. That is what gets us into messes like this in the first place."

"Stop trying to shift the blame," Bridget said. "I'm not sure why Fiona keeps insisting on this century, but Liam is the reason the attack is contained. If it hadn't been for him, the walls would have been breached. But the men who are responsible for the attack have to be captured."

Both sisters leaned toward each other and started arguing back and forth until they sounded like a swarm of angry bees. The candle flames in the chandelier overhead quivered in response, and the flames in the hearth flickered as though they too felt the rise in tension in the room.

"Are they saying what I think they're saying?" Logan whispered. " 'Doors through time' just took this reenactment to a whole new level. Cool. These sisters have a vivid imagination. But what is this Brigadoon place they keep talking about?"

Irene had no idea how to spring time travel on him; she was having a hard enough time reconciling it herself. She concentrated on the Brigadoon topic. Keeping her voice low, she said, "It was the name of a movie in the 1960s, one of my mother's favorites. *Brigadoon* was a story about a village priest who had protected his people from the evils of the outside world by his prayers and sacrifice. The villagers would sleep for one hundred years, and when they awoke only a day would have passed. My mother watched the movie so many times she knew the songs and dialogue by heart. I think Stirling Castle is under a similar enchantment."

Irene stared at the candle flames in the chandelier until her vision blurred. If her mother had taken this tour, that had to be why she was so obsessed with the movie. Or was there another reason?

The muscles along Logan's arm tightened. "Well, my favorite movie growing up was *Star Wars* because my father and I saw it together at least a dozen times. After we leave Scotland, we should hop on a spaceship to the planet Tatooine. You know, the home planet of Luke Skywalker, where…"

She leaned her head on his shoulder. She knew he was trying to lighten the mood again, something she was learning to appreciate about him. "I know about Tatooine, and I also know how crazy this sounds."

He kissed her on the forehead. "Good. At least I'm

not the only one freaking out. A lot of my friends believe Atlantis was a real place, and that a race of alien space travelers built the giant heads on Easter Island. All that stuff seems tame compared to an enchanted-castle theory, but at the end of the day, all this is just make believe."

"But what if it isn't?" Irene said. "I mean, you said it yourself. We might never know things like why the heads on Easter Island are larger than life size or if Atlantis existed."

The corners of his eyes crinkled as his mouth twitched in a smile. "Cool. The Death Star is real."

Irene fought back a grin as she elbowed him gently. "And you said I was the one with the hidden nerd flag. I suppose you attend comic book conventions."

"When we get back to reality, I'll show you my costume."

"You're joking?"

He lifted an eyebrow.

Chairs scraped over the floor as the sisters stood. Lady Roselyn remained silent for a moment, as though making sure she had everyone's attention, and then took a deep breath. "We have decided that you both deserve to know the truth. All of it."

Chapter Thirty

A smoke-filled haze settled over the windowless chamber, adding to the gloom. Irene wound her arms around her waist, feeling as though the walls were closing in. Whatever was going on had Lady Roselyn and Bridget worried. When Julia first announced that they really had dropped into the thirteenth century, Irene had dismissed it as the way Julia was coping with her heartache. Irene should have pressed Julia for more details when she had the chance.

Lady Roselyn stuffed her hands into her bell-shaped sleeves and raised her chin. "You are correct. The men who escaped our dungeon are the same troublemakers Logan confronted in the Matchmaker Café. The fact that Sam is helping them is worrisome, as well. He will have to be dealt with. They all will. But that's not the worst of it. When the wedding was delayed, the enchantment that protects Stirling Castle began to unravel. I think that is the reason it was so easy for Sam and his friends to convince the warring clans to abandon their truce and attack us. I honestly don't know what will happen next." She sank down, holding her head in her hands. "I need chocolate."

Logan leaned forward. "Okay, this might sound obvious, but why can't we just walk out of here? In case you missed it, my mother's not well. This place seems to agree with her for the moment, and for that my father and I are eternally grateful. But it can't last. She needs to be under a doctor's care."

Irene felt Logan's growing concern. He was correct. Right now his mother looked fine. That would change as the disease progressed. Ann would lose the ability to care for herself. Even though her family would do whatever was necessary, it wouldn't be enough. Irene wanted to stay at the castle until she learned why this place was so important to her mother. Watching Logan and knowing what he must be going through, it no longer mattered. They had to return.

"I agree with Logan. We need to go back as soon as possible."

"I wish it were that simple," Lady Roselyn said. "We can't leave. None of us can. When we traveled back in time, everyone on the tour became part of the story and therefore subject to its rules. The most important rule is that no one from our century can leave until the stroke of midnight and then only after there has been a wedding. Without a wedding…"

Logan stood, toppling over his chair. It crashed to the ground as he narrowed his gaze. "Hold on. Rewind. What do you mean, we traveled back in time? You're joking, right? That's just a story line. It can't be real."

"Please sit down."

"Not a chance. Explain."

Bridget slid a glance toward Lady Roselyn, who gave a slight nod.

"We're not your standard-issue matchmakers," Lady Roselyn said. "Our methods are a little unorthodox, but right now the bigger issue is that we're running out of time to fix things."

Logan's face looked ashen as he righted his chair

and sat down. Irene slipped her hand into his and felt him squeeze her fingers gently. Somehow it didn't feel as scary when he was beside her. She'd been faced earlier with the possibility that they were in the thirteenth century, so she'd had time to process the idea. Logan was trying to make the leap in a matter of minutes.

"Running out of time. That's an understatement," Bridget said under her breath as she rubbed her sister's shoulders.

Lady Roselyn patted Bridget's hand, their heated discussion forgotten. "We believe it's not enough to provide a romantic setting for couples to meet. That only checks off the physical attraction box. The real test for a couple's compatibility occurs when they are out of their comfort zone or in the face of conflict. How a person deals with conflict tells their true nature. Most couples don't really know the person they've married until they are faced with a conflict: the birth of a child, loss of a job, or death of a loved one. We provide both a romantic location and the added twist of conflict. In the case of the Stirling Castle experience, we stage a mock attack to test couples' reactions to danger and how they work together to overcome that danger. Our system is not without its challenges or failures, but we are proud of our success rates."

"We have this little arrangement," Bridget continued when Lady Roselyn nodded toward her. "We have permission to use Stirling's portal or door to the past, as long as we respect its enchanted rules, and one of those rules is that a wedding *must* take place on Christmas Eve."

Lady Roselyn pushed to her feet. "And since this

enchantment requires that a wedding take place on Christmas Eve, only then will the doors open and allow us to travel back to our own time. We had it all planned. Angus and Caitlin were to get married. As you are aware, they now are not speaking to each other. We approached Julia and Grant, and although they have made the transition from friends to a potential couple, they feel their relationship is still too new." Lady Roselyn drew herself up to her full height, looking more like Queen Elizabeth the First than a friendly tour guide. "We're desperate. We'd like you to take their place. We want you to get married."

Irene and Logan stood up so fast their heads bumped together.

"Marriage," Irene said under her breath, gingerly pressing on the sore spot.

She bent over, holding her stomach. "I can't breathe."

Logan stood beside her as though frozen in place as he slowly rubbed her back.

In the background, Lady Roselyn was talking on as though she'd just announced the next course at a banquet. "You two are made for each other. I've rarely seen a couple more in love with each other at first sight than you two. Marriage is the next logical step."

"The next logical step," Irene managed through gulps of air, "would be for Logan and me to get to know each other better."

Logan pushed back his hair with both hands. "Agreed. But more to the point," he said to Lady Roselyn, "marriage is an important step. I should know. I was married before. Messy divorce. Hurt feelings on both sides. Not pretty. There has to be another way."

Irene felt the room spin. She shut her eyes as she tried to regain her balance. Logan was divorced. He was not perfect after all. *Okay, don't overreact.* Divorce happened all the time. *No need to panic.* Guys left. Cheated…

"Are you all right?" he said.

"Why did you get a divorce?"

"We were married for only a short time before we realized it was a mistake."

"Children?"

Logan grinned. "She called me a child. Does that count?"

"That's not an answer. And this isn't funny."

Lady Roselyn approached Irene as though she were a small animal that could frighten easily. "Everything will work out. You will have the choice of several lovely gowns. The wedding feast is prepared. Guests have arrived. The musicians are in place. The Great Hall is decorated."

The wedding planner list continued, but Irene blanked out for a minute, holding onto the sides of the chair.

Bridget cleared her throat, drawing Irene's attention. "Give it up, Roselyn. This isn't going to work. Unlike us and the matchmakers in our family, people like Irene and Logan can choose whom to marry. We can't force them. It must be their decision. And don't forget that if Fiona suspects that they're not ready, she'll…"

"We are beyond doing what Fiona thinks is best. Besides, I suspect she would be perfectly fine staying here. There's something going on with her that I can't quite put my finger on. The bottom line is that we need a wedding, and Irene and Logan are made for each other."

Irene shook her head, repeating what they had said about Julia and Grant. "It's too soon."

Bridget put her hand on Irene's shoulder. "As much as it pains me to say it, my sister is right. At least consider it. There's more to the enchantment than a wedding requirement. It's also the reason Logan's mother looks healthy again. It protects those here from disease for as long as they stay. But if the balance is not restored, I'm not sure if even that aspect of the enchantment is still possible."

"You must wed," Lady Roselyn interrupted. "Otherwise we might not…I mean we may all be…that is to say…"

"We'll be stuck here," Bridget finished. "As in permanent residents of the thirteenth century."

Chapter Thirty-One

Irene had convinced the sisters that everyone deserved to know their lives might change, and the word was sent out to gather the tour group in a secluded area of the Great Hall. Lady Roselyn and Bridget were nearby, trying to bring a sense of normalcy to the castle after the attack. Irene had chosen a secluded corner where she, Logan, and Fiona could discuss what was happening and how best to bring up the castle's similarity to Brigadoon. While everyone trailed in, it gave her a chance to process the whole marriage question. This was a big step, no matter the circumstances. Did she even want to get married?

After she'd dumped her ex-fiancé, she'd lived in a date-free zone. Not because she was afraid of getting hurt again but because she was concentrating on her career. At least that was her story. Even Irene knew the arguments she'd made were weak. She'd considered getting a dog or cat to keep her company. She had settled on a plant.

Coming on this trip was the first real vacation she'd had in over a year, but she'd almost bailed. Her sister must have sensed her reluctance and had appeared on her doorstep the morning of the flight. Irene was fearless in the courtroom and a strong advocate for her clients. She trusted her instincts in everything—except when it came to relationships. She had known from the start that she and her ex were not right for each other. Had that been the real reason she'd dated him? Because she'd known all along that they wouldn't last?

Irene glanced at Logan. He had joined his parents when they arrived, but when she met his gaze he gave her a wink. A flutter of butterflies took off in her stomach, and she knew she was grinning like a girl with her first crush. Being around him felt like the first day of spring after a long cold winter.

She kept that feeling wrapped around her as the last of the tour group arrived. Sam was the only one unaccounted for, and soon everyone would know the reason.

Lady Roselyn and Bridget said that Fiona was the best person to explain what was happening, under these circumstances. Irene wasn't so sure that was correct, or if the two sisters felt it was time their younger sibling had a taste of what they were going through.

Fiona was off to the side. She had removed the sword she'd worn when the castle was under attack, but she'd kept the dagger. Julia, Grant, and Logan were standing by the window, while his parents were seated and holding hands. Ann and Sean looked like they were in a world of their own, one filled with warm autumn days and moon-kissed nights. They looked so happy, Irene felt guilty that the matchmakers were about to spring this news on them.

Logan joined her, kissing her gently on the cheek. "Sam didn't come. My dad said no one has seen him."

"Did you tell your dad what happened in the dungeon?"

"He said he wasn't surprised. He'd thought there was something off about the guy."

"Your dad is a great judge of character."

Logan glanced toward his father. He and Logan's mother were huddled together in deep conversation. "He knows people. He really likes you, by the way."

Grant and Julia had angled over to Logan and Irene. Grant peered outside through the shuttered window. "It's quiet out there."

Julia threaded her arm through Grant's. "Do you think we're safe?"

"We're safe for the time being," Fiona announced, drawing everyone's attention.

Her words ignited a buzz of conversation. The tension spoke volumes. It was clear a few of them already doubted the attack had been staged.

Fiona spoke above the din of anxious voices. "Thank you for coming. We thought you all should know what is going on."

"But I thought Lady Roselyn already told us what happened," Sean said, putting his arm around Ann's shoulders. "The attack was part of the performance."

Grant grunted. "I've attended a lot of medieval festivals, and I guarantee that there was nothing scripted about the attack on the castle. The men who attacked us were out for our blood. Scripted performance, my cherry red…"

Julia elbowed him in the ribs. "Grant's colorful comment aside, I agree with him. People in the castle are on edge. The attack took everyone by surprise. There was an attack when I was here before, that much about what Lady Roselyn said was true. This one was different, however. Last time, no one was injured, and the arrows weren't on fire; they just bounced harmlessly against the outer walls. Afterward, the sisters brought out tankards of sweet cider and we toasted our victory."

Grant nodded. "That confirms the stories Sam told us he'd learned from the friends he met online." Grant looked over his shoulder. "Sam should have been here by now."

"I doubt Sam will show his face," Logan said.

"Sam's part of the problem," Irene added.

Julia slid an accusatory glance toward Fiona. "Have you lost control over the story?"

Taking a breath, Fiona let her arms drop to her sides and moved to join the group. Her lips thinned as she nodded slowly. "You are right to be concerned." She briefly retold the story of Brigadoon, explained how a similar enchantment surrounded Stirling Castle, and then filled them in on the three men they'd locked in the dungeon only to have them freed by Sam. After answering a few questions, she continued, failing to keep the trembling from her voice. "To satisfy the rules of the enchantment, a wedding must take place. Until this tour, we've never failed. Caitlin and Angus…well, if they do reconcile, it will take more than a few hours, and we don't have the luxury of time."

Grant shuffled his feet. "If a wedding doesn't take place, what is the big deal?"

Julia's voice was a dry whisper. "Angus told me that if there isn't a wedding, all of us will remain in the thirteenth century."

Shock robbed everyone of a response, plunging them into silence.

Fiona held up her hand. "That is only part of the problem. We chose this short window in Scotland's history because it is peaceful. We're pretty sure we know who is behind the attack. The troubling piece is how they were able to accomplish an attack of this scale."

Grant shook his head. "Sam used to say he was related to a member of the Douglas clan and planned to visit them when he arrived. I thought he was bragging."

Fiona took a deep breath, her face going pale. "Suspecting the Douglas clans are involved is troubling. If Sam and his friends knew the identity of the leaders of the clans in this area and the weaknesses in the castle, they might have been able to incite them to violence. We have to find a way to stop them."

Chapter Thirty-Two

The meeting left an unsettled taste in everyone's mouth. The only conclusion was that Sam and his friends had to be stopped. What was left unsaid was what to do about a wedding.

The sisters had left Irene and Logan alone after they'd made one more plea for them to wed. Irene sat beside Logan in silence in their balcony overlooking the Great Hall. Irene had come to think of this spot as theirs. Fresh-cut tree boughs were draped over the rim of the balcony's railing. Their pine scent created a forest-like retreat that shielded them from the frantic hum below.

Logan took her hand in his and rubbed his thumb gently across it.

She knew Logan must be thinking about the consequences to his mother. No one could deny that she was getting better, but if there wasn't a wedding, would all that change? What would Irene have done if she had thought there was a way to reverse her mother's cancer? Just about anything, was the swift response.

She turned toward him. "There are only a few hours left until midnight…"

He let go of her hand and leaned his elbows against the railing. The boughs crushed under his touch and sent the fragrance of a forest wafting toward her. The smell was crisp and clean and clear. She edged toward him, knowing in that moment what must be done.

"What if Bridget is right, and this place is healing your mother? And if that weren't enough, there's a real chance all of us will be stuck here in the thirteenth century. I know that last part sounds very romantic. You'll get to learn how to use a sword. I'll get to wear long flowy dresses. Of course, there aren't any bathrooms or showers." She paused, going for Logan-style humor. "On the bright side, maybe you're the one who'll invent rugby. You could name it *Logan*."

He tilted his head toward her and laughed under his breath. "Wouldn't that be something? Very tempting. I'm not sure where the name originated, but men and women have been playing ball games long before Greek and Roman times. I think the first official rugby match was in Scotland in the 1850s. If I was stuck here forever, a rugby team would be top priority for sure. Who knows? It might take over as the national sport, knocking out European football. But you didn't want a history lesson on the sport. You were about to make a point."

She swallowed, gathering her courage. "The only solution is for us to get married."

He laced his hands together, and glanced toward the activity below. "Are you always this logical?"

"I know you've reached the same conclusion." She allowed the words to settle around them. She'd opened up the idea for discussion. Some might say they'd be marrying for all the wrong reasons. But how could that be the case, if the reason was unselfish? And then another argument broke through. "But you heard the sisters. It has to be true love, the kind that will last forever."

"One of my friends is in an arranged marriage," Logan said, still focused on what was happening in the Great Hall. "He's from India, and his family is very traditional. He's a neurosurgeon, and all he asked was that his bride have a similar family background and education level. He got his wish. She's a pediatrician, and he looks at her in the same way my dad looks at my mom. I know not all arranged marriages are successful, but neither are the other kinds. To love someone is to take a leap of faith."

His words settled around her like a warm cloak, shutting out the clamor of activity below. She didn't know how her mother had felt about her biological father. Her mother never mentioned him other than to say he'd died before Irene and Louise were born. Irene, however, had seen firsthand the relationship between her mother and stepfather. It was comfortable, companionable. Her mother had seemed content, and her stepfather had spoken only loving words about her. Movies and books spoke of opposites attracting or passions generated by volatile relationships, but that was the movies; this was real life. As it had for Logan's friend, love bloomed in many ways.

Feeling it was time he knew more about her, she let her words tumble out in a rush. "I knew my fiancé five years before we got engaged, but I don't think I ever really knew him or what he wanted out of life. I broke it off with him a few weeks before this trip."

"My wife and I were high school and college sweethearts. The marriage lasted a whole nine weeks." His mouth tugged at the corner in a bitter smile. "It looks like we've blown out of the water the theory that long courtships make for successful relationships."

Laughter erupted between them, easing the tension, but it dissipated as quickly as it had begun. Silence weaved around them until the lack of sound was deafening.

Logan glanced over at her, his gaze intent. "Will you marry me?"

Irene drew in a breath. "Yes." Then shook her head. "Whoa, that came out fast. When Chad asked me, I didn't give him an answer for two weeks."

Logan squeezed her hand. "Since you answered me right away, I'm guessing that's a good sign."

"What about your parents? What will they say?"

"They already think you're perfect and gave me strict instructions not to mess things up. They'll be thrilled."

Irene leaned against his shoulder as silence descended around them again. "What if this doesn't work?"

He didn't respond.

Chapter Thirty-Three

A half hour later, Irene and Logan's announcement was met with relief. But quicker than she could say, "Haggis is gross, no matter how much gravy is slathered over the top," the sisters had switched topics and devised a plan to find Sam and his friends.

And Irene hated every aspect of their plan.

"The sisters' reasoning is medieval," Irene said, mumbling to herself. Temper flashed through her as she paced in front of the hearth in the Great Hall. "The men are searching for the bad guys while we are stuck here."

Lady Roselyn had cancelled all the celebrations. But since the castle lacked central heating, a fire had to be maintained. And this one roared and attacked the wood with angry flames, which matched Irene's mood perfectly. The men had metaphorically patted her, Ann, Julia, and Caitlin on the head and announced they were going out to save the day.

To make matters worse, Lady Roselyn had suggested the women occupy their time feeding the fire and doing needlework. Seriously?

Ann and Julia had their heads bent together over a square of embroidery, while Caitlin was adding another log to the fire. She hadn't said very much except that she and Julia had bonded over their shared belief that Angus was a world-class loser. Caitlin was the only one amongst them who was from the thirteenth century, so maybe she'd think Irene was overreacting to being left behind.

Irene gritted her teeth. She was through with caring about what people thought.

She spun around. "Am I the only one who's spitting mad? The men are outside hunting that trio of cave dwellers while we're sewing. I hate sewing."

"Lady Roselyn said we should stay here." Julia stabbed a needle into a section of cloth she'd been embroidering. She grimaced as the needle pricked her finger. "Finding the troublemakers is man's work."

"Please tell me Lady Roselyn didn't actually say that?"

Julia sucked the blood off her finger. "Lady Roselyn said the first part. Grant added the second. He's in character, and he believed it made him sound like a knight protecting his damsel in distress. I have my own thoughts on the subject."

Irene crossed her arms over her chest. "I don't know about you, but I'm as angry as a nest of hornets. We may be stuck in the thirteenth century, but we're twenty-first-century women. We can help."

Ann muttered a colorful oath under her breath as she threaded a needle. Julia and Caitlin turned toward her with conflicting expressions of shock and humor. Irene wasn't surprised. Although Ann looked the part of the wise, beautiful, and refined duchess in a Regency novel rather than a curse-wielding mercenary in an action movie, there was a quiet strength about her.

Ann laced her fingers together in her lap. Outwardly, the way she held her hands looked innocent enough, except the knuckles shone as white as ivory piano keys. "Women in the thirteenth century were pretty fierce themselves. Who do you think defended the castles when the men folk trundled off on their grand adventures? What is more, who do you think made sure there was food on the table, and the sick were cared for? I know my husband and son. They'll find these men eventually. That's one of their strengths. But our intruders are hiding, and as the sisters said, we don't have the luxury of time."

The clarity of Ann's thought process was exciting. It was also spot on. Irene brought her chair closer to Ann's and motioned for Julia and Caitlin to do the same. "We keep referring to the intruders as Neanderthals, me included. We've underestimated our enemy. They're not as dumb as everyone seems to think. After all, they escaped a dungeon and somehow managed to persuade the clans in the area to launch a surprise attack. They'll suspect that the sisters have ordered their capture and of course go into hiding."

"I'm not so sure about the last part," Caitlin said. "They wanted to come on this tour. The attack could be their way of proving to the sisters that they belong here. I think I know where they are. One of the kitchen staff said he saw them hanging around outside when he went for wood."

"We could lure them to us," Ann suggested.

Julia's eyes widened. "Have you forgotten that they tried to kill us? I may not like sitting here turning my fingers into pincushions, but I know my strengths, and chasing after armed men is not one of them. Let Ann's son and husband and the others do their job. I just want to get back to civilization. After this, if Grant even suggests a reenactment festival, we're so over."

Ann leaned against the back of her chair. "Maybe

Julia's right."

"Except we're running up against a deadline," Irene said. "Everything is on hold until they're captured. No celebrations and, more importantly, no wedding. Without a wedding, we won't be going back. We're stuck in this century. I don't like the idea of luring them here any more than you do, but we have to do something."

Ann shook her head slowly. "Sun Tzu, who wrote *The Art of War*, had a famous saying: 'Know your enemy.' Do we know their names, or why they came here in the first place, or why they've attacked us?"

Caitlin poked the logs in the hearth with a fire iron. "Their names are Cory, Dave, and Alex. They are foulmouthed braggarts who do not understand the first thing about chivalry." She gave the logs another shove.

Julia set her needlework aside. "I know those names. They were on the same tour I was on before. They're computer programmers from a tech company in the States. They are not, however, the shy, nerdy types that turn out to be interesting and nice and even sexy once you get to know them. They're the creepy stalker kind, more interested in getting drunk, picking fights, and grabbing your…well, you get the idea. Sam said he had meant to meet some gamers here that he'd met online, but they'd been turned away. I should have connected the dots sooner."

Irene turned toward the hearth. The fire crackled, spitting embers and casting a glow over the crossed swords and shield hanging over the mantel. She reached up and touched the shield as an idea formed.

"It sounds as though they are here for revenge or, as Caitlin suggested, a second chance," Ann said.

Irene nodded, bringing her attention back to the group. "I agree. They've been denied their fantasy world and must be feeling pretty frustrated by now. Instead of cancelling the celebrations, we need to take them to the next level. Make it a party they can't resist. If they're convinced that our men are outside on a wild goose chase, they might risk coming inside. When they do, we'll be ready. Ann, do you think you can convince Lady Roselyn to resume the celebrations?"

Ann stood, so excited her eyes sparkled. "That might just work. When I'm done, she'll think it was her idea."

"Good. Now all we'll need is a way to invite them that won't draw their suspicions."

"I'll go," Caitlin offered. "All four of them tried to get me alone. Angus came to my rescue. He might not be the one-woman type, but he takes protecting women seriously. Despite my protests, and Angus' intervention, they are deluded into believing I'm interested in them." Her expression puckered as though she'd bitten into a sour lemon. She shuddered. "I'll tell them we've convinced the sisters to give them a second chance."

"Do you think they'll believe you?" Irene said.

Caitlin shrugged. "Cory, Dave, and Alex will want to believe it's true, and Sam's ego matches the size of his big head. They don't see themselves as bad guys. I'm sure they think this has all been a big misunderstanding."

"We'll both go," Julia said. "I don't want you facing those creeps alone."

Irene liked the way the plan was developing. They were all working together. "And I'll ask Fiona and

Bridget to follow you in case there's any trouble. Meanwhile, I'll set our trap in motion. We'll all meet back here in an hour."

Chapter Thirty-Four

The ambush was in place, the invitation sent, received, and accepted. Weapons were hidden and a rope tied to a nearby pillar. They were ready. Irene pressed her hand against her stomach. She felt like her first time in court. She'd thrown up her breakfast and lunch, then.

The man who'd first seen Cory, Dave, Alex, and Sam outside the kitchens confirmed they were advancing toward the Great Hall. She'd asked him if he could get word to Logan about their ambush plans, but she hadn't heard back from him.

Ice-cold panic flashed over her skin. Getting the men here was only part of the problem. Distracting them long enough for the plan to unfold was the bigger challenge.

Throughout the last hour she'd been so busy with the preparations—gathering weapons, rope, and linking together sheets of chainmail until her fingers felt raw— that she hadn't had time to worry. Waiting was the worst part. A chill rushed over her as though she were standing in a blizzard in a bathing suit. The sisters had made it clear. If they failed, everyone would not only be stuck in the thirteenth century for the rest of their lives, they'd be under constant attack by neighboring clans or the English. Not a cheery thought.

She glanced toward the balcony overhead. A

couple of hours ago it had been the place where Logan proposed. Now it would play a pivotal role in the ambush. Julia, Caitlin, and Ann had helped Irene link together suits of chainmail that Lady Roselyn had provided, plus the ones Irene had taken from the knights' statues near the library. They'd sewn the pieces together into a solid panel and attached one end of it to the railing on hooks. Their plan should work…in theory.

Ann rushed forward, out of breath. "The man from the kitchens says they are close."

"Did he hear from Logan?" Irene asked, her pulse racing.

Ann shook her head. "He saw Logan and his men heading away from the castle, but they were too far away for him to reach them without alerting our targets."

Footfalls echoed through the corridor, announcing the intruders more effectively than the screech of trumpets.

Irene ignored her churning stomach as she waved to Fiona, Bridget, and Ann on the balcony and then signaled for the musicians to begin. The sisters had proven to be very helpful and had enlisted the kitchen and castle staff to participate in the deception.

The Great Hall transformed as people took their positions near the hearth. They pretended to play board games or gathered in the center of the room to dance. Ann moved amongst them, helping to keep everyone calm and on task. To the casual observer, the hall looked like a postcard image of the perfect Christmas Eve celebration.

The men's footfalls grew louder. One of the

fiddlers struck the wrong note. Irene's heart raced. Obviously she wasn't the only one on edge.

Julia grabbed Irene's arm. "They must know they're walking into a trap."

Caitlin shook her head. "I don't think so. They were so excited we extended the invitation, and even congratulated each other on accomplishing their goal." She frowned. "They want to play Fiona's version of blind man's bluff. I almost gagged."

Irene felt an idea bloom to life. She smiled. "Well, if it's blind man's bluff they want, then their wish is our command."

She signaled again. The music got louder. People clapped in time to the melody, increasing the noise level as Ann led them in a Christmas carol. The laughter sounded strained, but Irene hoped she was the only one who would notice.

In the next instant the men appeared in the archway. They'd exchanged their costumes for clothes that were more accurate to the thirteenth century. Irene no longer thought of them as mice. They were big fat rats. They stumbled forward in an intoxicated fog, their eyes too bright and their conversation too loud. Caitlin had assessed their motivations accurately. Their main goal was to participate in the matchmaker's celebration, and in their haze of ego, they'd convinced themselves that their orchestrated attack on the castle would be rewarded.

They advanced as though they intended to walk past Irene and her friends, but Irene was prepared. Julia and Caitlin stood on either side of Irene; forming a loose semicircle. Acting as one person, they moved forward, preventing the rats from coming any closer.

The man Caitlin had identified as Alex was out in front, while the other two stood on either side of him, forming a triangle. Sam held back, shifting his gaze past Irene. She couldn't tell if he expected an ambush or if he was anxious to join the party. Regardless, the men were spaced too far apart for their plan to work. They needed to stand closer together.

Irene pasted on a smile and unwound a red silk ribbon from her hair and waved it back and forth in front of her. She felt silly, but her distraction worked. The men shifted toward her. Their gaze followed the path of the ribbon like a tennis ball at a championship match. "Are you ready to play a game of the sisters' version of blind man's bluff?"

"About time," Sam said, easing to the front of the group. He jerked his head toward the men, and they all nodded like bobble-head dolls.

Caitlin cast a flirtatious look at Sam and performed a graceful curtsy. Smiling, she sank slowly to the ground. Sam couldn't keep his focus off Caitlin, and his comrades were equally as entranced. Mesmerized, the men closed ranks and moved forward as though joined at the hip. When Caitlin rose, she also dangled a ribbon. "We will have to bind your hands, as well."

Again they nodded, swept up in the moment and the possibilities.

"Please turn around," Irene said in her best seductress imitation. "We want to blindfold you."

It was as though her words were infused with magic. The moment she'd finished speaking, all of the men spun around and placed their hands behind them. They were so accommodating, Irene almost felt sorry for them. Almost.

146

The trap was set. Irene and Caitlin rushed to bind their hands.

Cory whined that the ribbon was too tight, but Sam told him to "man-up."

When all the men were bound and blindfolded, Irene raised her arm and shouted. "Now."

Music ceased. The strained conversation and laughter came to an abrupt halt. Everyone moved into position.

Metal scraped against the railing of the balcony as the sisters released the solid panel of chainmail. It rolled down the side, ending inches from the floor. The entrance was sealed as Ann led her group forward.

"What's that noise?" Sam slurred.

"Part of the game," Irene shot back. She and Julia grabbed the rope tied to the pillar. Working as a team, they raced around the men as they began binding them together.

Dave squeaked out a protest. Ann shoved a gag in his mouth.

Sam raised his shoulder to the side of his face and managed to ease his blindfold up. "What's going on? We just wanted to play a game."

Caitlin reached for a crossbow and leveled her weapon. "Only men and women of honor are allowed in Stirling Castle."

His eyes widened. "You can't…"

Irene stuffed a wad of cloth in his mouth. "We just did."

Irene stepped back and let the others finish securing the men who'd caused so much trouble. She felt like someone had thrown open a window and let in the sun. "We did it."

Ann looped her arm through Irene's and smiled. "I can't wait to tell our men that their damsels in distress caught the bad guys."

Chapter Thirty-Five

A short time later, Irene was still smiling over Ann's words as she changed her clothes for the Christmas Eve celebrations. The men had all returned and helped lock up Sam, Cory, Dave, and Alex. When that was done, they confirmed that the neighboring clans were abiding by the truce. Lady Roselyn had more good news. She and her sisters gathered everyone together in the Great Hall and made their announcement.

A wedding was taking place after all. A roar of excitement spread through the Great Hall and reached a fever pitch when she added that everyone needed to change into fresh clothes that fit the festive occasion. After all that had happened, people were ready for a party.

The matchmaker sisters had transformed one of the spare chambers off the Great Hall into a fantasy world of gowns, jewels, and veils. The clothes glowed in vibrant greens, golds, blues, reds, and silver so bright they outshone the stars. Tiaras inlaid with sapphires, emeralds, and diamonds rested on velvet cushions, next to displays of semi-precious stone pendants, necklaces, earrings, and bracelets. It looked as though someone had transported the crown jewels of England to Stirling Castle.

Lady Roselyn informed them that brides seldom

wore white, as color was a sign of good fortune. And as an added bonus, for tonight's celebrations they could forego wearing the thirteenth-century headgear.

Julia exchanged her red gown for one in a shade of blue the same color as Grant's eyes, while Irene smoothed her hand over the green velvet confection she had chosen that was so beautiful she felt like she was the queen of a small kingdom. She added a pair of emerald earrings and selected a narrow gold crown for her head. It was a little indulgent, but tonight was made for dreams.

Irene twirled in a slow circle, mesmerized by how the fabric caught the candlelight. She felt more alive than she had in years. Her heart swelled. She wouldn't have met Logan if she hadn't sought answers to the pendant and her mother's secrets. Had her mother guessed all along that this could happen?

There was something about this place. It was more than the time travel aspect—it was the whole atmosphere that the matchmaker sisters had created. The distractions of the outside world had melted away, helping bring clarity to the lives of those who had open hearts. The crushing symptoms of Ann's disease had disappeared. She was clearheaded and laughed often, and Sean said it was as though they were both young again. Julia and Grant seemed to grow more in love by the second, and she and Logan...

She smiled like a child on Christmas morning, then glanced around to see if anyone had noticed her standing in the center of the room, smiling like a fool. But she wasn't the only one in a holiday mood. Julia was humming and trying on tiaras, and Ann had discarded her black dress for one that reflected the bridal gowns in the thirteenth century, a rich burgundy silk embroidered with gold and silver threads. The fabric shimmered when she walked, as though her dress was lit with tiny lights.

Sean had given her a jewelry box, and she'd opened it and touched the ruby pendant that hung from a gold chain.

"May I help you put it on?" Irene asked. When Ann nodded, Irene lifted the gem from its nesting place. "The necklace is stunning."

Ann touched the fire-red stone and whispered, "The glowing ruby should adorn those who in warm July are born." She smiled. "A silly saying, I know, but Sean found it while we were still in school. He loved that rubies were my birthstone." Ann showed Irene her wedding ring: a princess-cut diamond surrounded by rubies. "His favorite saying was, 'A person wearing a ruby would never doubt that they are loved.' "

Irene finished clasping the necklace and came around to face Ann. "That is one of the most beautiful sayings I've ever heard."

Ann's laugh was fresh and clear, like water over a babbling brook. "I think he made it up, but I never said so. In our case, at least the saying fits." Ann smiled again. "You mother's locket is lovely."

Irene touched it protectively. "Fiona called it that, as well, but it's only a pendant. There aren't any seams."

Ann's smile was gentle. "I recognize the style from my research books. The seams are hidden behind the spokes of the snowflake. If you like, I can show you how it opens."

Irene nodded slowly as Ann slid the tip of her

fingernail into an almost invisible seam. The lid popped open, and Ann's smile spread like morning sunshine over a meadow. "What a charming couple, and the gentleman is so handsome."

Julia peered over Irene's shoulder. "I can see the resemblance. Is he your father?"

Irene felt as though a breeze had swept over her skin. The woman in the picture was her mother, and she was dressed in the same gown as the one in the portrait Logan had discovered. And Ann was right. There was a resemblance between herself and the man in the picture. If this was her father, why hadn't her mother shown her his picture?

Lady Roselyn peeked her head into the room. "We're about to begin. Come along, ladies. You don't want to miss your wedding."

But Irene and Logan weren't the bride and groom. Lady Roselyn had declared Sean and Ann were renewing their vows. Sean attributed the miracle of Ann's healing to the enchantment of Stirling Castle and said that if they left, Ann's Alzheimer's would return. They vowed to make every moment count. Logan was his father's best man, and Ann had asked Irene to be her maid of honor.

Logan announced he'd wanted to make it a double wedding, but his mother had intervened, saying Logan and Irene should start their life in the present. Ann was right, of course, but Irene was surprised by the disappointment that washed over her and mentally took herself to task. After all, she'd just met the man. They hardly knew each other.

A crowd had gathered and was waiting expectantly. On Lady Roselyn's cue, bagpipes began a traditional wedding song, "Scotland the Brave." The notes infused the air with the haunting melody of the tragedies and triumphs, sorrows and romance that were the history and strength of Scotland. Ann clasped her hands in joy, and Julia gave her a hug, but Irene felt rooted to the floor. Avoiding what Julia had said about the picture, Irene concentrated on taking slow, even breaths.

The melody vibrated through her, the music a strange exclamation mark to Julia's words. *Is he your father?* In a numbing trance, Irene helped Julia fan out the train on Ann's gown.

"Are you all right?" Julia whispered.

Irene jerked a nod. "Bagpipes. The sound caught me off guard."

Julia motioned to the pipers as they marched in place waiting for Ann. "Or maybe it was one of those men playing the bagpipes," she said with a grin. "I didn't know Logan played."

Irene snapped her gaze to the group and saw, sure enough, Logan was one of the pipers. He winked, and his eyes crinkled in a smile as Ann took her place. Fiona handed out garlands of graceful strands of wheat dusted with gold and crystal-like snowflakes made from sheets of silver foil. She directed Irene, Julia, and Caitlin to stand behind Ann. Once everyone was in place, the procession turned in the direction of the castle's interior Chapel Royal.

Laying her bundle of golden wheat in the crux of her arm, Irene stepped in behind Ann. Irene's thoughts flew about her in a thousand different directions at the same time, even as she concentrated on the music, on taking one step at a time. Was Julia right? Was the picture in the locket of her father? But even as she revisited the question, she knew the answer. The portrait she'd seen of her mother proved she was at Stirling Castle and had participated in the sisters' tour. The picture in the locket proved that her mother had met someone. Was the man Connor? The man her mother had mentioned in her diary? Why hadn't her mother stayed? Was her father still alive? Why had her mother kept it a secret?

Irene stumbled.

Logan was at her side, his hand on her arm, as the procession weaved past her. His expression was a vision of concern.

"I'm fine," Irene mumbled.

"No, you're not."

"Please. Go on without me," Irene said.

He gazed toward the procession as it turned down a corridor. "One less piper won't be missed."

"But you're the best man. Your parents…"

"They will understand. Tell me."

Her eyes blurred as she covered the locket with her hand. "I think my father was here, and that my mother and he…"

He wiped a tear from her face and smiled. "They found love, if only for a short time. That's very romantic."

"But my sister and I never knew him. Why didn't she tell us? Was he part of this century? Why didn't she stay?"

Logan shifted the weight of his bagpipes and threaded his arm around her waist, drawing her to him. His kiss was a feather-soft promise. "Your parents had their reasons for keeping their secrets. Maybe that's why your mother only gave you her diary after she'd died. Maybe she was afraid she'd be judged for falling in love. I believe it's enough to know that they loved each other. Don't you?"

Chapter Thirty-Six

Was it enough?

The wedding ceremony was a blur. Irene was swept along over the waves of celebration. The merrymaking of the reception was in full swing, and Irene felt like she was now coming up for air. She'd kept hold of the locket, afraid to let it go.

Lady Roselyn drew in beside her. "You discovered the secret in your mother's locket. I'd always wondered. From the date on the portrait, she would have participated in a tour with either my mother or my aunt. But that much we already suspected."

The bright notes of harps, lutes, and fiddles rang in Irene's ears. "But you knew she was here."

Lady Roselyn folded her hands at her waist. "After our last meeting, my sisters and I researched our records. Your mother fell in love with someone from this century. It happens sometimes. Your mother would have had the choice to stay, of course. It would have been impossible, however, for a man from the thirteenth century to leave."

Irene fought back the well of tears that gathered in her eyes. "Is he alive?"

Lady Roselyn placed her hand on Irene's arm. "Our records indicated your mother was here several times. The matchmakers believed it was because she was always searching for her soulmate. We now believe she had already found him. According to the accounts, she spent a lot of time with a man named Connor."

Irene cleared her throat. "My mother spoke of Connor in her diary."

Lady Roselyn nodded and continued. "The two of them were so careful no one guessed. There was a notation of an attack on the castle, much like the one we experienced. It didn't go as planned. There were casualties. After that attack there is no record of your mother returning."

The last words hung in the air and caught on the soft notes of the harp as the melody faded. Irene's eyes brimmed with hot tears. "Connor didn't make it."

Lady Roselyn squeezed Irene's shoulder, confirming Irene's statement.

One of the performers took his place in the center of the Great Hall, and his deep baritone voice captured everyone's attention. The melody seeped into Irene, filling her with a sense of peace.

There was no denying that the picture in the locket was her father. The resemblance in his smile and the shape of his eyes was unmistakable. Her mother had kept his identity a secret. She'd met and fallen in love with a man from the past. Irene managed to smile. Before she arrived here that idea would have sounded ridiculous. Now it just sounded…well, romantic.

Irene fingered the locket as her vision blurred. Her mother had given her and her twin sister pictures of their father in their matching lockets. Parting gifts. There was also the entry in her mother's diary, an entry that Irene had committed to memory. Until today, it had seemed borderline crazy. Now it made complete sense.

Dear Diary,

My daughters would never believe me if I told them who, or rather when, their father and I met. They will have to experience the magical place of Stirling Castle for themselves. Seeing is believing, as the old cliché goes. If there is anything I'd want them to remember when they discover my secret, it is that Connor and I embraced love. There are no regrets. I wish the same for my daughters. May they find a love that will transform their lives. A love that will stand the test of time.

Irene had read those words more than once, but for the first time it seemed like her mother was saying them to her directly. A message from mother to daughter and friend to friend. All the puzzle pieces were falling into place.

Perhaps the journey to Stirling Castle wasn't as much about her mother as it was about discovering a way to learn how to move on. Irene might never learn all the secrets her mother had guarded, but maybe her mother had had her reasons. Not all secrets were meant to be told.

From across the Great Hall, Logan stood gazing over the crowd. Dressed in a red tartan plaid, he scanned the wedding guests again, and she knew. She knew he was looking for her. Her heart beat faster. She knew she was smiling. Knew she was moving toward him as though nudged from behind.

His smile when he focused on her made her feel as though she were the only one in the room. She'd known him for hours, not even days or weeks, and yet... Was that how her mother had felt when she'd met Connor?

Irene's face warmed as Logan strode through the Great Hall as though it were empty and they were the only ones present. A few in the dancing circle glanced toward him. Those in his direct path stepped aside to let him pass.

And then he was standing in front of her. Waiting.

The tempo of the balladeer rose as others joined their voices to his. When Logan reached her side she felt out of breath. "We know so little about each other," she said.

"We'll figure it out together." He paused and took her hand in his. "You should always wear green. The color matches your eyes."

Figure it out together. The words rang like sweet music. She smiled. "And you should always wear a kilt."

He laughed. "It was my dad's idea. He found a collection of them in one of the rooms. He said this is our family plaid, the proud Mackinnons. I tried to tell him that this style of kilt wasn't popular in Scotland until much later, but he dismissed my objections. He said I shouldn't worry about the Wikipedia police. My mother added that men look good in kilts and that was reason enough to wear them."

"Your mother is a wise woman, and your father a lucky man."

Logan nodded and put his hand on Irene's shoulder, turning her toward the circle of dancers. Enveloped in his arms, she leaned into him. The Great Hall vibrated as couples sang along with the ballad or joined in the folk dances. Grant had asked Julia to dance, and Fiona was standing near Liam.

Logan's mother and father were holding hands like young lovers and laughing and singing along with the rest of the dancers. They nodded toward Irene and

Logan and then snuggled together.

"She looks like a different person," Irene said. "They both do."

Logan drew her closer against his chest, and wrapped his arms around her waist. "They look exactly how love should look."

"I'm not sure what we do next," she admitted.

"I am."

He got down on one knee and held out a ring.

Her pulse raced as though she'd been running a marathon. Running to keep ahead. Running to find happiness. Maybe she'd been running all her life and was just now learning how to stop.

A hush fell over the hall, and Irene glanced over her shoulder. The fiddlers had put their instruments down, and everyone was watching them. Why was he doing this? It was no longer necessary. The requirements of the enchantment had been fulfilled. They didn't have to get married. Disappointment once again churned in her, taking her by surprise.

She cleared her throat and leaned toward him, lowering her voice. "There was a wedding. The sisters said we don't have to worry. Everything is back to normal. You don't have to ask me to marry you."

His smile warmed the air around her. "I know. That's why it feels right. I want to marry you. I meant it the first time, and I mean it now. I'm asking you in front of my parents, in front of witnesses, and with the ring that belongs to my mother." His smile faltered. "But if it is too soon…"

Her heart thundered. "Yes. I mean, no, it's not too soon, as crazy as that sounds. Yes, I'll marry you."

Logan slipped the ring on her finger. It was a

perfect fit.

He rose in one fluid motion, his eyes locked on hers, and cupped her face in his hands, pausing for a brief moment as though memorizing her features. Then he leaned closer, a breath away. "I've loved you from the moment I first saw you."

"I love you…"

Her words trailed off as his mouth found hers. Warmth swirled around her, and he held her as though he would never let her go.

Chapter Thirty-Seven

Lady Roselyn sat at her desk, waiting for Fiona to arrive. A short time ago, this room had been transformed into a fantasy world where guests could select the clothes from a different time and place and dream. While the wedding vows were being exchanged and guests gathering for the reception, everything had been put back the way it was. All the gowns had been returned to their wardrobes, and all the jewels locked safely in vaults. But the chamber looked sad, somehow.

She tried to shake off the impression. She should feel relieved. Happy. The tour was almost over, a wedding had taken place, and couples had found their soulmates. Mission accomplished. But she was on edge as though reflecting the mood around her. Nothing about this tour had been routine. She should be thankful that it was almost over, instead of wondering if this was a sign of things to come.

She bent over the thick matchmaker book, with the symbol of a Scottish thistle etched in its leather cover. The entries dated back hundreds of years. It was customary that the eldest sister record the matches made in the Highlands, and carrying on the tradition brought her a measure of peace.

She dipped her pen in the inkwell and added Irene and Logan's names beneath Ann and Sean's and Julia and Grant's. From time to time she would make a point to check on her couples and update their status. It was part of who she and her sisters were. They wanted everyone happily settled. For now, Lady Roselyn was pleased with her couples' progress. She'd already written the word "married" in the column next to Ann and Sean and felt confident she would be doing the same for the other couples soon.

Finished, she leaned against the chair and rolled her shoulders. Even with the tour's successes, she couldn't shake her unease. What was keeping Fiona? Lady Roselyn pushed back from her desk, stood, and began pacing the room. That sister of hers had no sense of time. One day she'd cut it too close and...

"Bridget said you wanted to see me?" Fiona had entered from a side door. Her face was flushed and her breathing labored.

Lady Roselyn took in Fiona's appearance. She looked perfect in every way. There wasn't a hair out of place, as though Fiona had stepped out of a thirteenth-century fashion magazine. A pillbox-style hat sat on her head, secured with a chin band. Her hair was neatly secured under a gold net at the nape of her neck, and she wore a loosely fitted gown under an embroidered surcoat.

Their mother had often said that it was the little things in a person's appearance that hinted at either inner peace or rebellions bubbling beneath the surface. In Fiona's case, Lady Roselyn speculated on the latter. Fiona was trying too hard to avoid arousing attention...or suspicion. There was nothing peaceful about Fiona's expression or her bearing. She reminded Lady Roselyn of a coiled spring.

Lady Roselyn tested her theory. "You look lovely."

Fiona slipped a finger beneath the chin band to loosen it. "I thought it was time I started looking like the other maidens in this time period."

Lady Roselyn fluffed out her sleeve. "Pity we won't be coming back for a while."

Fiona's expression froze. She chewed on her lower lip. "If it's about the troublemakers, we've taken care of them, and we've made sure there was a wedding. Customer satisfaction is at an all-time high." Her voice hardened. "The Matchmaker Council can't blame us for what happened. In fact, they should give us ribbons."

Lady Roselyn forced herself to remain calm. Fiona had overreacted. Not good. It shouldn't matter where they conducted their matchmaking tours. It bothered her that she'd had to resort to deception to ferret out the truth, but she had tried the direct approach a few months ago, and Fiona had deflected her questions. Fiona would go missing for hours on end. Lady Roselyn had to know the truth. Being the eldest was a heavy burden. There were days…

She cleared her throat and pressed her point. "We haven't heard from the council regarding what happened here. I'm being proactive. Besides, we could use a change of scenery. It will do us all some good."

Fiona loosened the chin band at her neck even more, then gave up and removed her hat. "We have to come back."

The expression in Fiona's eyes spoke of longing and pain. Lady Roselyn glanced away for a brief moment, recognizing that expression. She'd seen it often enough in her mirror. She tucked the matchmaker book under her arm. The signs had been there all along. Of late, her younger sister was more excited than usual to visit this century. She knew for a fact Fiona wasn't meeting with her betrothed. Liam often commented that he couldn't find her. Lady Roselyn suspected her sister was seeing someone in this century. Normally she liked being right. Now was not one of those times.

Lady Roselyn kept her voice light, as she reached for Fiona's arm. "Staying away from Stirling Castle for a while will be for the best. You'll see."

Fiona looked like a trapped animal. Her gaze darted behind her as she tried to disengage from her sister's grip. "I think I forgot something. It won't take long. I'll be right back."

Lady Roselyn held firm. "There isn't time. The door to the twenty-first century has opened, and we have to escort our guests back to their own time." She launched the final test. "When we return, we can start planning your wedding. You have delayed it for too long as it is. Have you and Liam decided where you want to get married?"

"Liam and I don't love each other."

And there it was. Her heart ached for her younger sister. She'd hoped love would grow between Fiona and Liam. It hadn't happened for her and her late husband, but that didn't mean it couldn't happen for others. Lady Roselyn repeated the speech her mother had given her on her wedding day. "Arranged marriages are based on other considerations. Marriage between matchmakers has never been about love. It's about carrying on our traditions and helping others find their soulmates."

"Do you ever wonder if it's time we challenged those outdated rules?" Fiona said.

Lady Roselyn guided Fiona over to the door. "Never," she lied.

Chapter Thirty-Eight

Back in the dressing room of the Matchmaker Café, Irene took her time changing from the thirteenth-century gown to her twenty-first-century clothes. Their return to the twenty-first century was anti-climactic. All they had to do was walk through a door. There was a little discomfort. A flash of light, blinding cold, and, of course, mist, but all she kept thinking the whole time was that she didn't want to leave.

Irene draped the gown over her arm. It was heavy, inhibited movement, and was impractical, but it represented the new awareness she'd learned about herself and those she loved. No one was perfect, and that was okay. She'd spent her life on the fast track, moving from one perceived crisis to the next. There was an old cliché that advised people to "take time to smell the roses." She hadn't known there were roses to smell. The enchantment of Stirling Castle had forced her to slow down and examine her life.

She touched her mother's locket and whispered her gratitude. She felt as though a weight had been lifted from her heart, allowing the sunshine to rush in.

From across the room, Lady Roselyn smiled in her direction. She finished talking with Julia and crossed toward Irene. Lady Roselyn had also changed into modern clothes, but she still managed to look regal. "It's hard to let go," she said when she reached Irene.

"I'm sure you hear that often."

Lady Roselyn's mouth pulled into a thin smile as she accepted Irene's gown. "Not often enough. Some people are not ready to accept love. Some, like Julia, and Grant, need a nudge to recognize their friendship has bloomed into something more. The most difficult to reach are those who either have unrealistic expectations or who don't feel they are worthy of a great love. My sisters and I welcome the challenges that come our way. Matchmaking is our calling, and we believe there is a match for everyone." She draped Irene's gown over the arm of a chair nestled beside a table, and reached for something on the seat. "You are one of those who will take the spirit of this place with you always. We have a gift for you." Lady Roselyn produced a large box, wrapped in plaid paper and decorated with snowflakes cut out of silver foil. Inside was a Christmas mug, a canister of hot cocoa, and a container of chocolate sprinkles. "So you'll never forget us. Now, off with you. You have a man waiting."

****

Outside Stirling Castle, Christmas bells chimed in the distance. Along the curb was a bank of taxicabs. They stood in rows like polished black domino pieces, all shiny and new. The storm had passed, and the sky was clear and studded with stars. The light reflected off the snow as though it were coated with the dust from thousands of diamonds.

Participants from the matchmaker tour were headed toward the taxis. The men who'd caused so much trouble were being escorted to a police car. Irene knew they'd been given two choices. One, an overnight stay in the local jail, or two, try to explain where they'd

167

really been and risk a permanent stay in padded cells.

Julia, holding hands with Grant, waved to Irene and blew her a kiss goodbye before climbing into a taxi.

Members from the other tour began filing out of the café, as well. The family made up of the mother, son, and father who'd been so obsessed with their cell phones before the tour, now walked together hand in hand. The tour leader's group followed closely behind him like ducklings waddling after their mother. They were talking over the top of each other in their excitement to share their experiences. Many were holding hands, a few had their arms entwined, and in between the chattering laughter and smiles they paused to kiss their partners or hug their children. They may not have shared the matchmaker tour experience, but the sisters were right: Stirling Castle had woven its own brand of Christmas magic around all who entered.

"It's hard to let go."

Logan's voice was so much a part of her that she recognized it at once. She put her tote bag containing her mother's diary over her shoulder and slipped her hand in his. "I don't want to leave either."

He drew her into a warm kiss and whispered, "We'll be back for our honeymoon. I didn't think I'd ever find what my parents have. I was actually resigned. Then I met you."

Her heart filled with joy, and somewhere she heard bells ringing. "I feel exactly the same."

Still holding her hand, he hailed a taxi. "There's William. He's right on time."

Hands intertwined, they headed toward the last remaining cab. As they drew nearer, she wondered if she should bring up his parents. To no one's surprise,

Ann and Sean had asked the sisters if they could remain in the enchanted time of Stirling Castle. The sisters had said yes. But what must Logan be feeling?

He paused a few feet from the taxi. "You can ask."

"How did you know…?" When he smiled in response, she said, "Your parents looked very happy."

His expression seemed lit by an inner peace as he smiled. "They are the happiest I've seen them in a long time. They're like teenagers experiencing their first love, only knowing it's more than a crush: it's the forever-after kind. My parents are exactly where they want to be…and so am I."

The door to the taxi opened, and out popped the jolly driver who'd driven Irene to the castle. So much had happened that it felt as though days had passed instead of hours.

"You're right on time, William," Logan said.

William tipped his hat and winked at Irene. "I see the matchmaker tour worked out after all." Not waiting for an answer, William opened the passenger door. "Where would you two like to go?"

"Surprise us."

A word about the author…

Pam Binder is an award-winning Amazon and *New York Times* bestselling author. *Publishers Weekly* has said: "Binder gracefully weaves elements of humor, magic and romantic tensions into her novels."

Drawn to Celtic legends and anything Irish or Scottish, Pam blends historical events, characters, and myths into everything she writes.

Pam is also a conference speaker, writing instructor, and president of the Pacific Northwest Writers Association.

http://pambinder.com